YOURS TO SEDUCE

Karen Anders

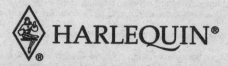

HARLEQUIN®

TORONTO • NEW YORK • LONDON
AMSTERDAM • PARIS • SYDNEY • HAMBURG
STOCKHOLM • ATHENS • TOKYO • MILAN • MADRID
PRAGUE • WARSAW • BUDAPEST • AUCKLAND

To Meghann and Briana—always reach for your dreams
And never, ever give up

ISBN 0-373-79115-1

YOURS TO SEDUCE

Copyright © 2003 by Karen Alarie.

All rights reserved. Except for use in any review, the reproduction or
utilization of this work in whole or in part in any form by any electronic,
mechanical or other means, now known or hereafter invented, including
xerography, photocopying and recording, or in any information storage
or retrieval system, is forbidden without the written permission of the
publisher, Harlequin Enterprises Limited, 225 Duncan Mill Road,
Don Mills, Ontario, M3B 3K9, Canada.

All characters in this book have no existence outside the imagination of
the author and have no relation whatsoever to anyone bearing the same
name or names. They are not even distantly inspired by any individual
known or unknown to the author, and all incidents are pure invention.

This edition published by arrangement with Harlequin Books S.A.

® and TM are trademarks of the publisher. Trademarks indicated with
® are registered in the United States Patent and Trademark Office, the
Canadian Trade Marks Office and in other countries.

Visit us at www.eHarlequin.com

Printed in U.S.A.

1

"DON'T YOU WANT TO TOUCH ME, Lana?"

Sean stood in front of her in the dim light of the fire station. Her heart jumped at the hot, sexy rasp of his voice—a voice fashioned for shadows and whispers.

He was dressed in just his uniform pants, the suspender straps tight against the hard muscles of his smooth, bare chest.

"Ah, Lana, I think about you, dream about you, want you...."

His face was in partial darkness. The lower half tantalizing, the full, sensuous lips, the strong jaw, and the smooth column of his throat bathed in shadows that pooled like dark, sweet chocolate.

Then he stepped into the full light and her breath caught. The gray eyes that regarded her were as deep and subtle and dangerous as smoke from a wildfire. His wheat-colored hair framed a face that was drop-dead gorgeous—stuff dreams were made for.

Lana could feel the blood roaring in her ears. Sean O'Neil, pal, buddy. She swallowed. Co-worker. Not smart, Dempsey. Not smart at all.

She shouldn't lust after him like this because she worked with him. But the bet she'd made with her daring girlfriends changed all that. One night with Sean would be worth the risk.

The savage need in him called out to her. The intensity about him frightened her even as it drew her. Erotic danger. She backed up, away from the smooth stalking grace of him.

She didn't answer, but every muscle throbbed in her at the seductive lights in his beautiful eyes.

"Do you want to touch me?" he asked with an odd desperation in his voice. Desperation and hope.

Lana had one glimpse of his gray eyes before his head descended.

It was a hot kiss, filled with hunger and need. It was pure and simple. He wanted her and she wanted him.

His fingers tangled in her hair, cupping her head. The kiss continued, scalding and consuming, seeming to suck her will from her. His tongue encountered no resistance as it swept with fervent insistence into the softness of her mouth.

His voice stole softly through the silence, his breath mingling with hers. "The taste of your mouth is so sweet," he said.

"I want you," she whispered fiercely. "From the first time I laid eyes on you, I've wanted you," she finished raggedly. Her eyes caressed his face, his throat, then moved back up to his burning eyes.

His scent enslaved her; the brush of his fingers against her throat was like licks of flame against her already aroused body. She shivered as she ran the backs of her fingers against his taut skin.

"I want to make love to you," she murmured, her mouth going to the moist, heated steel muscles of his chest, pressing her lips to his salty, musky flesh.

She kissed the exposed skin, trailing her fingertips along hard muscle.

When her tongue came out and licked his flat nipple, he moaned softly on an indrawn breath. She swallowed as excitement coursed through her. With a movement meant to savor, she couldn't help doing it again. This time gently sucking the hard nub.

Breathing hard, his whole body jerked, his head falling back, his eyes closing in sensual rapture that made Lana feel as if she were gripped in a tight, flaming fist.

Her breathing quickened at the powerful hardness of his sculptured body. She allowed herself a little bit of satisfaction when he pulled her tightly to him. As his hot mouth slammed into hers, his kiss demanded, overpowered and possessed her until the need for him was a starving ache in her bones.

The lights came on, but Lana couldn't stop kissing him. The sirens blared, the voice over the loudspeaker announced a fire in progress and still she couldn't let him go.

"Come on, Dempsey, up and at 'em."

Lana opened her eyes to find Sean close, but it wasn't in an amorous embrace. He was shaking her shoulder to wake her. Firefighters were jumping out of bed, running for the stairs and the bays where the fire engines waited.

"Dempsey. You okay?"

She nodded and threw back the covers, throwing off the heat of his hand against her bare skin. It wouldn't do for Sean to touch her now.

It was an unspoken rule that Lana and Sean didn't get too close. The heat between them would be too much. Lana wanted to change that. Had to change that because of the dare she had made with her two friends Sienna Parker and Kate Quinn. Now she was obligated to get Sean in bed and obtain a souvenir.

Sean O'Neill. The man who was her best friend, a man whom she played pool with and hung out with on Friday nights like one of the guys. He was her partner and treated her as if she were just another firefighter. And Lana would think that Sean viewed her like that, if she didn't catch him looking at her every so often.

With lust in his eyes.

In the split second that his hand stayed on her arm, Lana felt all the frustrating sexual urges come to the fore. No, it wasn't a good idea to have him touch her.

Not after that mind-blowing dream.

She swung her feet to the floor and right into the black rubber boots, pulling up and fastening the heavy canary-yellow overalls more commonly known as bunker pants.

The sound was earsplitting as Lana emerged into the engine bay where the big ladder engine was kept, along with the vibrant red pumper, glossy from the day's exhaustive cleaning.

Before taking her designated seat on the engine, she grabbed her turnout coat. It and the bunker pants, with three protective components, provided added defense against burns.

The equipment had saved her too many times from fatal burning for her to ignore any piece. She always placed safety first before comfort. Of course the equipment was heavy, but thanks to the stringent physical requirements of her job, she didn't even notice the weight. She hooked up the jacket without thinking about it and smoothed down the Velcro strip to seal it completely. After pulling on the no-mex hood, she grabbed her yellow helmet, jammed it on and tightened the chinstrap.

After climbing on the engine all within one minute, her gloves tucked into her equipment belt, she pulled the self-contained breathing apparatus or SCBA for short from its bracket behind the seat and shrugged into it.

As soon as the alarms had gone off, the doors to the firehouse began to open. The engines were now loaded with firefighters ready to do battle with an unpredictable and deadly enemy. In her experience, the darkness would only hinder this early Monday morning attack on the fire.

As the impressive ladder engine roared down the freeway blowing its loud horn, Lana listened to the details they were getting about the type of building, its construction, and the number of people who might be caught in the fire. It was close to two in the morning on the first day of her two-day shift and already they had what sounded like a serious one.

Against her will she looked over at Sean seated next to her, no doubt his thoughts also on the blaze.

She hoped this wasn't another arson-induced fire. A number of suspicious fires had occurred in San Diego in the last two months. And at the most recent one, she'd discovered the evidence of trailers and accelerants.

So far this firebug was more interested in apartment buildings than empty commercial property, but Lana took nothing for granted. The adrenaline in her blood urged the engine faster. Her body tightened in anticipation of what lay ahead.

When the big red rig arrived on the scene, Lana realized they were third in, which meant she would be on search-and-rescue detail. Standard operating procedure dictated that the first-arriving engine attacked the fire with tank water, the second-arriving engine laid a supply of lines to the first engine and the third-arriving crew performed necessary forcible entry, search, rescue and ventilation. Lana automatically was on the lookout for Battalion Chief Johnson for his specific orders, all her thoughts going to the task at hand.

Before she could get to the battalion chief, she heard a scream and her head snapped toward the direction of the voice. A woman ran right for her. She clasped Lana's arm in a death grip. She felt the strength of the woman's desperate hold even through the thickness of her canvas jacket. A policeman followed right behind the woman.

"Lady, I told you to stay behind the barrier."

"It's all right, Officer. Can I help you, ma'am?" Lana said, covering the woman's hand with her own. The woman's face was stark-white, her eyes wide and frightened looking.

"My Angie. Dear God, where's my baby?"

"What does she look like?" Lana asked the distraught woman.

"Curly hair, big blue eyes, and she's dressed in pink pajamas."

Lana turned to Sean, but he was already speaking into his radio. With quick, curt words he discovered that no one had rescued a child meeting Angie's description.

"What apartment?" Lana asked urgently.

"Apartment 3B on the third floor. My sister was

baby-sitting her while I worked. Please, please,'' she whispered, ''save them.''

Lana was already donning her face mask and striding toward the building, Sean at her heels. With a quick radio call to the battalion chief they obtained his permission to enter the structure. Every moment was precious; every moment lost brought the two victims one step closer to death.

It seemed that every available firefighter worked to contain the blaze so that the whole block didn't go up in flames. Truck 78 sat at the curb as Lana passed it. The motor whined as the hydraulic aerial ladder swept across the dark sky, expertly missing any overhead wires.

Lana heard the sound of breaking glass and as the ladder hit the roof, firefighters ran up the rungs carrying axes. Ventilation of the roof was the first step in fighting a blaze. Lana barely registered the sound of a chain saw and the splintering of wood as she rushed toward the entrance to the apartment building and the victims inside.

A large hose already filled with water snaked through the lobby door as Lana and Sean rushed in. She could hear them but didn't see the nozzle crew as she realized the stairs were still intact.

Sean was right behind her, a big, comforting presence. Thick black smoke made maneuvering difficult and finding her way even harder. They had thirty minutes of air to find the woman's sister and child and get back out of the building.

She moved up the stairs as fast as she could, the smoke so thick she couldn't see anything. When they reached the third floor, it was fully engaged—flames licked at the wood, paint curled and peeled, reducing it to ash in seconds.

The hose crew was fighting the fire and Lana and Sean moved down the hall away from the crew as they searched for 3B.

When they found the apartment, the door was locked. Ever mindful of the potential for a backdraft where carbon dioxide mixed with air could cause a violent explosion, she took off her glove and felt the wood.

It wasn't hot so she used her ax to break the lock. Pulling a latch strap from the equipment belt, she hooked it over the lock on the door. She was pretty sure that it wouldn't lock behind them but she didn't want to take any chances. She stayed near the wall, using a deliberate search and rescue procedure that had been drilled into her.

It took them precious minutes to move around a room that was filled with smoke. Whenever they found a window, one of them would swing the ax and break it to help with the crucial ventilation of the building.

When Lana bumped into the couch, she spied a teenage girl. She was unconscious, but breathing shallowly. Lana rolled the teenager off the couch onto the floor.

"I've got her," Sean yelled over the noise of the fire and the efforts of the firefighters to stop it.

"I'll look for the child." Then she went into the back bedroom. She removed her mask so that she could yell into the room. Acrid smoke stung her nostrils and made her cough. "Angie, where are you?"

No answer. She moved on and checked the first place children usually hide—under the bed.

She was lying on the floor facedown, a tattered brown teddy bear clutched to her. She turned and Lana could see fear and terror in the little girl's face. She was six, about the same age as her twin nieces.

"Sean, I found her," Lana called to Sean.

Lana reached out her hand. "Come on, sweetheart. Come to Lana. I'll take you to your mommy." She used her softest voice.

"I'm scared," Angie said firmly, clutching the teddy bear tighter.

"I know, honey, but I'm a firefighter. Come with me and I'll take you to her. It's okay. I won't hurt you. See."

Lana pulled off the helmet and handed it to her under the bed. Angie looked it over thoroughly, noting the SDFD emblem on the front. Relief now replaced the terror that had once been there. Angie crawled toward Lana and she pulled her out from under the bed, replacing the helmet and tightening the chinstrap.

"Where's Fluffy?" she inquired with panic in her voice.

"Lana! Hurry up!" Sean yelled.

Lana picked up the bear where Angie had dropped it.

Situating the little girl solidly on her hip, Lana covered her with a blanket she'd taken from the bed and wrapped her.

"Now, Angie, I want you to put your face in my coat and hold on to my neck really tight. I have to move fast so you don't get burned." She smiled reassuringly and tousled her curls.

"It smells funny," she protested, wrinkling her little pert nose.

"I know, honey, but it's important." She held the girl tightly.

Angie looked up at her with a solemn face and she smiled winningly. "Okay, Lana."

Lana tucked the blanket around the bear and stepped back into the smoky living room.

"Sean," she called out.

"Here," he said. "Come on!" Flames leaped at them hungrily as she and Sean emerged into the hallway. Making their way back into the apartment, Lana grabbed the radio fastened to the side of her turnout coat, depressing the button. "Chief, O'Neill and I are on the third floor with two victims. The hallway is inaccessible. We need a ladder.''

''Bedroom,'' Sean said as the door began to smolder and peel.

Lana turned to head in that direction. With a rushing sound, the upper floor caved in. Lana went into a crouch to protect the little girl. The minute debris stopped raining down, Lana called out, ''Sean, are you all right?''

She held her breath until she heard his faint reply. ''I'm okay. Looks like I'll have to chop my way through.''

''I'll help.''

''No. Get into the bedroom and get the kid out. Then come back.''

''I'll be back for you.'' She spoke into her radio again, ''Chief Johnson, O'Neill and a female victim are trapped behind debris from a caved in ceiling. He's going to chop through. I'm going to the bedroom to get the child out and then help O'Neill.''

''That's a go,'' Chief Johnson said.

Lana carried Angie into the bedroom. She set the child down. ''Stay down. Breathe evenly and don't panic. You're going to be safe.'' She immediately went to the window and leaned out.

''Dempsey,'' the chief's voice came over her radio. ''We see you, but can't access that window. Can you get to the next apartment?''

Lana gritted her teeth. "Yes. Get the ladder up and I'll get through."

Lana knelt down and checked Angie. Her eyes were open wide, but she was having difficulty breathing. "Hang in there, honey. Breathe."

Lana chose a place on the wall and gripping her ax, she struck firmly. Plaster sprayed, hitting her SCBA mask and bouncing off. Wood splintered and flew all around her as she relentlessly attacked the wall.

She turned to check Angie. When she saw the little girl's eyes drooping, she called out, but Angie didn't respond. Lana abandoned the wall, grabbed the little girl and shook her.

Angie's blue eyes popped open.

"Stay awake, sweetheart," Lana pleaded. She took her air mask and put it over the girl's face. "Breathe."

Lana replaced the mask over her face. She went back and started to attack the wall again.

The wall gradually gave way. As soon as she could see through to the other side, she went back to Angie, picked her up and ran at the partially open wall.

Crashing through, Lana landed heavily on her right shoulder. She went to the window. They were already wheeling the ladder into place. As soon as hands reached out to help her, she gave the girl over.

"She'll need an EMT. I'm going back for O'Neill."

Through the chopped hole in the wall Lana re-entered the bedroom emerging into the living room.

"Sean?"

"I'm almost through," he yelled. Lana once again swung her ax. The familiar sound of her SCBA whistling told Lana she had a quarter of a tank of air left.

She started to pant inside the mask, knowing that her exertion was using up the precious oxygen more rapidly.

When the whistling stopped, Lana doubled her efforts, her swings increasing at a rapid pace. She only had ninety seconds of air left.

Just when she felt blackness playing around the edge of her consciousness, she could hear Sean's efforts on the other side.

When she broke through, Sean grabbed up the girl. Lana gestured Sean ahead of her.

As Sean handed the girl through the window, Lana fumbled with her mask, going down to her knees. There was no air and her hands couldn't seem to grasp the straps to get it off.

"Dempsey?"

It was Sean's voice and she couldn't respond.

She started to black out, but he ripped the mask from her face.

Grabbing her under the arms he pulled her toward

the window. Pure sweet oxygen flowed against her nose and mouth and she breathed in greedily. When she opened her eyes, Sean was holding her up, his handsome face covered with soot and sweat.

Her heart turned over in her chest. On the job, she was always professional around Sean, never letting on about how she was feeling, but for a moment her emotions rose up and broke away from her control.

He stared into her eyes for that moment, and in them she saw the worry and the concern and something dark and tempting.

"Can you move? It's too hot to hang around here," he said, breaking the mood.

She smiled at him and nodded. "I'm fine. Let's go."

Lana climbed down the ladder, shocked to see how much of that floor was engulfed in flames. When she reached the bottom, the chief was there. He was eyeing the building and then looked at her. "That was a fine job, Dempsey."

She nodded at him and turned to find Sean at her elbow. "Nothing like cutting it close."

"You know me, O'Neil. Always on the edge." Sean laughed.

"Do you two need a breather?"

"No, sir," they replied.

"Take another line in," the chief said.

After going back for replacement SCBAs, Lana

beat Sean to the hose and, along with two other firefighters, headed for the building.

Smoke was now pouring out of the lobby doors along with a constant rain of water. The lobby was now engulfed in flames and while Lana turned on the hose, she wondered how that could have happened. But with no time to contemplate it, she forged ahead.

The building groaned and Lana looked up and saw cracks developing in the ceiling above her. Burning plaster began to rain down and then a huge chunk of ceiling started to fall. Someone hit her in the middle of her back and she went down, losing her grip on the hose. It started to serpentine like a snake as it whipped back and forth. She heard a thud and turned in time to see Sean fall. It was like everything was in slow motion. Lana didn't hesitate. She was up and moving, discovering that the other two men were down, too. She was able to rouse Smitty, a veteran. She grabbed her radio and shouted into it that the lobby ceiling was collapsing. Smitty grabbed one of the downed firefighters and lifted him into a fireman's carry.

Sean's head had been injured. She bent down and muscled Sean onto her shoulders.

It was no easy task. The man weighed a ton, all that muscle and he was tall to boot. He must be at least six-two to her five-nine.

When she got him outside and lowered him to the

pavement, she saw even more blood trickling down his temple. The gash was the only abrasion she could see. She checked his breathing and he was holding his own.

Another loud crash sounded at her back, but it barely registered with her. She never even looked over her shoulder.

She unbuckled the strap and removed his hard helmet. She worked efficiently and quickly.

"Sean," she said over and over. When his eyes popped open, Lana found herself staring into deep pools of intense gray.

Two paramedics came over and Lana backed up, letting them take care of Sean.

For a moment, she couldn't breathe. She just stared at him, her chest feeling tight. When he sat up, and insisted he was all right, a weakness buckled her knees.

But she couldn't give into it. It was an unspoken rule that firefighters never discuss their fear, especially for her. It would look weak to her fellow firefighters if she acted like a worried mother hen. Sean would never live it down and she'd be ribbed about it mercilessly.

A firefighter she didn't know came to stand next to her. He had soot on his face, but it was odd how his turnout coat and pants seemed brand-new.

"Way to go," he said softly, "That was awesome the way you pulled him to safety."

Lana could see the obvious look of respect on his face and she gave him a nod.

It was a nice gesture, but she didn't care what he thought about her rescue. It wasn't something that she had done for his respect. At this moment, all she wanted to do was touch Sean to make sure he was all right.

While the paramedic dabbed at Sean's cut, he searched around him. His eyes met hers. Experiencing the same rush of feelings she'd had only a moment ago, Lana found herself close to tears. They stared at each other for a few moments, releasing a funny fluttering sensation in her chest.

It was then she realized that she was going to follow through on seducing Sean. She cherished their friendship, but only now realized that experiencing physical passion with him was something she'd always felt was lacking in their relationship. Unspoken or not, she was going to have Sean O'Neill purely because she wanted him.

Relief washed over her and she let out a sigh to expel the tension in her body. He smiled at her then, a big, beautiful grin that lit up his handsome face and made her knees buckle all over again, but for decidedly different reasons.

She drew back suddenly afraid.

Blinking back the tears and stowing the overpowering urge to pull Sean into her arms, she turned away, went to the big red rig, gathered up another air tank and turned toward the fire.

Her work here still wasn't done.

MURMURS AND RUSTLINGS about the fire being arson filtered down to Lana. A firefighter breaking down the Fourth floor found a suspicious area in one of the apartments. There was evidence of flammable liquid called accelerants, which was substantiated by the clear burn line or demarcation on the carpeting where the arsonist set down trailers of the accelerant and ignited them.

Lana "knocked down" the fire ground including the tedious, but crucial task of checking all the burned materials for lingering embers. The debris would be put into a pile that would be pulled out later and dumped in the street. The remains of the fire would then be hosed down.

The call had come in at two o'clock in the morning and Lana's arms now felt like lead from swinging her ax and hauling debris. She'd been busy for almost seven hours. She was currently working in the basement, and as she paused she noticed spalling in the cement on one side of the basement. Spalling, which was cracked concrete, was caused by intense heat and it was odd that the basement would have shown any signs of that. A fire normally burned upward, not outward and never downward. Flames were drawn toward ventilation and followed fuel paths.

It could only mean that someone had started a fire in the fourth floor apartment and the basement.

Lana bent down and took a closer look at the charred area and knew that she'd been right. Someone had intentionally set this fire hoping that people would die.

Disbelief washed through her. Could she be reading the signs wrong? It was incomprehensible that a person would deliberately set two fires designed to keep the residents trapped and unable to escape.

She stopped her work and alerted the battalion chief who promised to pass the information onto the arson investigator.

But the whole incident left her feeling restless and unsatisfied.

Impatiently she continued to clean out the basement, waiting for the investigator to show up.

Finally he walked in and her heart sank.

Dane Bryant was a large man and came from the old school of firefighting. He didn't approve of women in the ranks and didn't hide that fact from anyone. He had the look of a bully about him, the kind of man who only sought out positions of authority to give him a sense of power over other people.

He grunted at her and she pointed to the area where she had discovered the spalling.

Dane bent down and examined the area while Lana watched over his shoulder. He shifted and blocked her view and a little tendril of anger sprouted in her.

She moved over so that she could see what he was doing.

"Dempsey, don't you have something constructive to do?"

His tone of voice was very clear. He doubted she could be trusted to change a lightbulb let alone be competent to spot signs of arson.

Eyes narrowed in annoyance, Lana said very succinctly, "Yes, Lieutenant Bryant, I have something to do."

He turned to look at her, his pale eyes narrowed.

"And what's that?"

"My job."

He snorted, clenching his jaw. "Well, I'm doing mine and I say you're wrong."

"It's spalled."

"Sure it is, but the fire was strong down here."

She used his words to strengthen her argument and insisted, "But how do you explain it? Fire never descends."

"This whole place collapsed. This fire was most likely caused by burning debris from above."

"Why not take a sample of the soil and test it for accelerants? This arsonist has come close to killing people. He's not going to stop now."

He stepped closer to her, an attempt at intimidation, but Lana held her ground never giving an inch.

"I know my job, Dempsey and can muddle through without your expert opinion." The mocking expression on his face made her anger burn hotter than the fire just extinguished. He would undoubtedly laugh at her if she lost control and smirk at her if she backed down. It was a no-win situation.

"If you give her enough time, Bryant, she'll browbeat you into complying."

Sean's voice penetrated the thick air and Lana moved away from Bryant as Sean came into her view.

"What will it hurt to take a soil sample?" Sean asked.

"Butt out, O'Neil. I don't need *you* and her ganging up on me." He brushed past Lana, making her stumble to the side.

Sean's strong arms reached out to steady her.

Something flashed bright hot inside of her, a pure reaction to the emotions, emotions she couldn't express. "I don't need you standing up for me like some big brother. I can fight my own battles."

Wrenching herself away, she walked out of the burned building, knowing that her anger was more directed at the fact that Sean felt she needed protection at all.

And she'd caught a glimpse of that white bandage against his dark skin. Her heart had wrenched in her chest telling her she still wasn't ready to pull Sean into her arms and start something foolish.

Their past relationship was one of keeping their sexual distance. Platonic friends they were not. Lana knew this. You didn't lust after a platonic friend and she *lusted* after Sean. He had never verbalized his interest in her, but a woman knew when a man was interested. It was an instinctive thing. Lana knew if she made any attempt to seduce Sean, he would cave into the seduction without much of a struggle.

The souvenir dare now added a whole new spin to a workable relationship. They could pretend to be friends and pals as long as they didn't give in to their baser instincts. The dare both excited her and scared her. She was moving into a new area with Sean and she wasn't sure that it was a good idea. But the thought of finally seeing Sean naked and having his body take hers was more than she could deny she wanted.

Sometimes, fighting fire was the least of her battles.

2

SEAN CAUGHT UP TO HER as she was stepping up to the rig to sit down. She was exhausted and dirty. She was angry with not only Sean and Bryant, but herself as well.

She didn't look at Sean as he settled next to her.

"Why didn't you go home or to the hospital?" Her tone was belligerent as if she was trying to start a fight. Sometimes it was easier that way. Her feelings often surged to the surface at the end of a tough fire. They were hard to contain. The things she saw could haunt her for days unless she blew off steam.

Hiding her emotions from a man she wanted to get into her bed wasn't easy. Lana was a straightforward person and said what she thought most of the time, but with Sean she held back. Their relationship wasn't just man to woman or firefighter to firefighter. They were friends and had been friends for years. Had she always had a crush on him or had it developed? She couldn't remember when she'd gotten these feelings for him. Perhaps she'd always had them.

"Leave a fire? No way. Besides, I was fine, just a little bit of a headache."

She knew exactly how he felt. To leave a fire was sacrilege. To leave a fire and not make sure that all the bases were covered bothered her, too. The fact that Bryant had pushed her suspicions aside because he didn't like women firefighters was troubling, too. This shouldn't be about gender. It was about saving lives and catching whoever was setting these fires.

The thoughts chased themselves around in her head and Lana knew that she was going to do something about it. Bryant could go to hell.

When the engine pulled into the station, Lana jumped down and cleaned her tools, checking and restocking her belt. Sean worked close by, but Lana didn't engage him in conversation. She still felt too raw with emotion to speak. If she'd been going off-shift, she would have headed over to talk to Sienna or Kate, but that wasn't possible.

It was best to shower, eat and sleep since she'd be on duty another twenty-nine hours. Not a bad schedule most of the time, Lana liked the two days on and four days off.

The showers were coed and afforded no privacy, so Lana had to wait until the men were finished before she could take hers. Lana simply put a sign on the door when it was her turn.

Distracted, Lana didn't realize that someone was still in the showers, until she heard the water come on. She had already taken off her grimy clothes and with honed reflexes she grabbed up her towel and wrapped it around her body, tucking the end in snugly between her breasts.

That's when she saw the discarded pile of clothes. She recognized the badge on the shirt. Glancing back toward the door, she realized that they wouldn't be interrupted. The dare reverberated in her head. She had pushed her friend Sienna to go after her hot Navy SEAL. How could she back down now and miss an opportunity to take what she wanted from Sean?

She approached the open stall and her breath caught. He stood with his back to her, the powerful muscles of his torso gleamed under the heated spray of the shower.

Her eyes moved down lower, unable to stop the sudden need to see every inch of his virile strength. Fat rivulets cascaded down his wet, gleaming skin, over the thick muscles of his powerful buttocks, tangling in the golden whorls of hair covering his legs.

Steam eddied and curled around the misty bathroom from the hot flowing water. She breathed, ''Oh my,'' unable to tear her eyes away from the magnificence of his muscular body. She forgot to swallow, or breathe, or blink, gaping at him, as if he were an alien creature. Obviously hearing her whispered explicative, he stilled, his back muscles taut and sleek. He turned and the movement brought her gaze to his smoky eyes, flaming brightly.

His luxurious blond hair was slicked back off his face, the locks dripping water over his broad shoulders.

She watched in fascination. The droplets slid tantalizingly over the molded contours of his pectoral muscles, down over the rippling strength of his stomach, disappearing into the dark hair at his groin. Her eyes remained there, her pulse jumping in rapid succession, her breathing increasing into little puffs, desire curling inside her. Her breath caught in her throat when she saw what her scrutiny did to him.

She should leave. She should back up and walk out of the room, but even as she thought it, she couldn't follow through.

She wanted him, she thought quickly, and her body answered with a thrumming response over which she had no control. But fear grew in her, a fear of herself, her emotions, her heart.

She could see the desire in his eyes. His arousal had been instantaneous, just from having her eyes on him. She was playing with pure, unadulterated fire, and she had no business standing here ogling him as if he were hers.

Yet, she was supposed to make him hers for a bet. He grinned at her, a slow grin that turned her stomach to mush.

"Lana? What are you doing in here?" he whispered in a voice laced with surprise and what she thought sounded like pleasure.

The words beckoned her to him, a man whom she'd wanted for years. She had to acknowledge that to herself. She wanted him for what seemed like forever.

She moved toward him caught in the magnetic pull of his body and eyes, the promise of his lips.

As she drew close to him, she could feel the warmth of his body. "Lana?" he asked in a thick voice as if he were strangling.

She swallowed and realized she was holding on to the terry cloth draped around her body in a death grip. She loosened her fingers and released the towel.

Sean lunged forward. "Lana, no," he cried, his big hand wrapped around the unraveling cloth.

The backs of his knuckles nestled in the valley between her breasts. His touch set off chaos in her chest, sending her heart into a breath-stealing lurch. Her nipples tightened into hard nubs, the wet towel arousing each hot peak.

"Why not?" she whispered back, afraid to ask it any louder.

"So many reasons," he replied as if in agony. "We work together. We're friends. It would complicate matters," he commanded softly.

"I was thinking the same, but if we got the sex

thing over with maybe my skin wouldn't tingle every time I see you."

"Lana," he groaned.

"I want to touch you." Lana closed her eyes, overwhelmed by the need to do more than touch him.

"I want you to, but..." he said in a rough, low voice.

She caught her breath. Ignoring the *but,* she reached out and touched his damp skin. The moment her fingers made contact, she wanted to press the flat of her palm to all that hard muscle.

With need coiling inside her, she slid her fingertips around his well-defined pectoral muscles.

There was something in his eyes, something that threatened to rip free. She wanted it and was also terrified of it. She knew it because it was exactly what she felt. For one long moment, the battle raged inside her—logic against need. If she moved forward, just a fraction of an inch, she could have something she was yearning for, aching for.

They were caught in each other's gazes, a scant inch apart. If she moved away, the towel would fall. If he moved away, the towel would fall. *She* had no intention of catching it. Something more powerful than common sense pulled her toward him, heated her blood, drew her eyes to his mouth. That lush, full bottom lip beckoned to her. Then she noticed the wound on his forehead. The bandage was gone,

taken off for his shower. The powerful emotions
rushed back and she reached up to gently touch the
skin around the injury.

She'd wanted a taste of him from the moment
she'd first laid eyes on him, and now, as the heat
between them intensified, she couldn't think of a
single reason not to take that taste.

She trailed her fingers down his scratchy cheek,
along the taut cords of his neck. Bringing her other
hand into play, she pressed both flat against the
heavy muscles of his chest, trailing her hands along
the thick ridges of muscle delineating his abdomen.

He released the towel with a harsh groan as the
back of her hand brushed the tip of his cock. As the
terry cloth fell away, Sean caressed every inch of
her nakedness with his eyes. It felt decadent and
dangerous to stand before him free of all that heavy
clothing they wore every day. Freeing to finally let
him know that she wanted him.

"I must be out of my friggin' mind."

His lack of sanity didn't seem to stop him. He
stepped closer to her, his big, rough hands cupping
her breasts.

He bent his head and his tongue snaked out.
"Sean," she whispered, begged. His mouth closed
over her and she arched wantonly into the heat of
him. She moaned his name again. The sound of it
reverberated against the tiles, throwing his name
back at them.

He sucked hard, and she cried out in raging hunger for more.

When his head raised, her lips parted slightly and Sean read the action for what it was, a silent invitation. She pushed on his chest backing him into the spray of warm water and he pulled her with him.

The water splashed down over her skin, warm and wet, sliding over her skin like liquid silk, a cleansing, heated waterfall.

Dropping his mouth to hers, he pressed his full, sensual lips against hers. Even with her confidence that what she wanted was him, a warning bell sounded somewhere in the back of her mind. One time wouldn't be enough it clanged, not nearly enough. But desire swept through her like a flood and drowned the alarm, leaving nothing but incredible sensations in its wake. He tangled his fist in her dark hair and tilted her head back, giving him better access, a better angle.

Lana fell against him as the strength in her legs ebbed. She gasped at the shock of their bodies coming together, at the surprise pleasure of his lips touching hers, and he slid his tongue slowly into the warm, wet cavern of her mouth. He kissed her slowly, deeply, with a lazy insolence that made the act as intimate as sex.

She pulled him closer, gasping in the feel of his mouth, the hot water pounding her sensitized skin. At that moment she knew nothing about prudence.

The desire rising up blocked out all else, letting instinct take control. She sank against the hard, muscular planes of his body, shivering at the feel of her breasts flattening against his chest. He swept a hand down her back and over the ripe curve of her buttocks, cupping her, lifting her into him, and pressing her close against the erection that was hard, yet silky against her stomach.

Lana trembled and groaned, barely aware of the sounds she made. A dozen different emotions ripped around in her like leaves in a storm wind. Every nerve in her body was jumping with life. She couldn't remember the last time a man had touched her like this, made her want like this. And with nothing more than a kiss. It thrilled her and frightened her and made her burn for him.

He took control, pressing her back against the wall of slippery shower tiles. She cupped his face as his kisses got deeper and stronger, more frantic. Her hands went into his whiskey-colored hair. Her fingertips massaged his scalp as his hips pressed against hers, his pelvis thrusting against her with wild abandon.

Her hands curled over his shoulders, sliding around to his back as she urged him as close to her as he could possibly get. Her hands continued their adventurous exploration when she reached for him and cradled his hardness in her hands. His face pressed into the hollow of her shoulder and he groaned softly as she caressed him wonderingly, amazed at the strength and sensuality encased in that hardness.

"Lana," he begged huskily.

She had every intention of complying. It took her only a moment to grab the foil packet from her cosmetic case that she had purposely carried with her in the hopes of getting Sean alone. When she came back, she moved down his body an inch at a time, kissing his chest, abdomen, the jut of his hipbone, and the tops of his thighs. On her knees she was at the perfect level for his straining cock.

As her mouth closed over him, he stiffened, both hands pressing against the shower tiles, his breathing ragged. Lana explored his strong length with her lips and tongue, licking away the streams of water, an endless task, as the shower continued to provide more. Long minutes passed until Sean became too restless with need. With two hard hands, he pulled her up and fastened his mouth to hers savagely.

All finesse was gone, the thought of control laughable. He pressed her against the tiled wall, branding her with his body. She couldn't get close enough; she couldn't feel enough. His mouth was everywhere and had a direct relation to her ability to stand. His warm avid tongue swirled the droplets from her nipples, then paused to suck deeply, causing Lana to cry out at the sharp sensation. One hand smoothed her flat stomach then tangled in the wet hair at the juncture of her thighs. His intense desire ignited her own, and she cried out at the exploring finger he sent inside her.

"Sean," she whispered, almost incoherent with need, but she didn't have to be more direct, because Sean knew exactly what she wanted. What they both wanted. He grabbed the condom out of her hand and sheathed himself.

He placed both hands beneath her bottom and lifted her against the tile. Her legs encircled his waist, and he entered her with a surge that drew a moan from both of them.

"You're so hot, Lana, so damn tight." He gasped, his hands at her hips directing their movement. His eyes were slitted open, and he watched in satisfaction as Lana reacted in pleasure. The sight of him watching her pleasure made her back arch away from the wall. He drew one nipple into his mouth. And then it was too much for both of them. He pressed her to the wall again; her legs tight around him, and powerfully thrust up inside her over and over until they both cried out in unison.

Long moments later Lana became aware that the water running over them was cold. Sean released her, and she put her feet on the floor, grateful that he didn't completely let go of her.

He held her against him as if he couldn't seem to let her go and a giggle slipped out of her.

Sean moved away so that he could look into her face. "This isn't funny."

"I know. It isn't funny at all."

Sean closed his eyes and leaned his forehead against hers.

"Are you surprised, Sean?"

He once again looked down into Lana's face. "Yeah, I guess I am. I thought we were friends."

"We are friends."

"Now we're a little bit more."

"Yes, we are."

"I don't want sex to muddle everything else."

"It doesn't have to."

"Yeah, but it does."

Lana moved away from him into the spray of the water, washed her hair and soaped her body quickly. When she was done she turned to look at Sean. He was watching her; that same hungry look back in his eyes.

"You're a damn beautiful woman," he said raggedly.

Before she could answer, a booming came from the shower room door.

"Jeez, Dempsey! Are you going to use up all the hot water? The grub is ready!"

"Keep your shirt on! I'll be there in a minute!" she yelled back, irritated at the interruption.

She walked over to where she'd placed her robe and shrugged into it.

Sean grabbed her arm and hauled her up against him. "You are something else. Do you have nerves of steel?"

"They wouldn't dare come in here while the sign is on the door."

His mouth came down on hers, his lips still wet, his body damp. Droplets from his hair dripped on her cheek, but she didn't care. She wrapped her arms around his neck and kissed him back.

When they finally parted, Lana reached up and gently touched his cut. "You should get another bandage on that."

He nodded. "Thanks for saving my life."

There was something in the gruff quality of his voice that got to her, and Lana found herself suddenly struggling against a thick wad of emotion. She clenched her eyes shut and swallowed hard, nearly overcome with feelings for this man. Feelings that caused a painful ache deep inside her.

"I was terrified," she said in a small voice. "I wanted to wrap my arms around you."

He pulled her closer as she released a breath. Rubbing his hand down her spine, hugging her hard, he said, "Can you imagine how big that would have gone over? We would never have lived it down."

"No."

"And if we're discovered in this shower together like this, we'll get more than ribbing, Dempsey."

"Right." A rush of fear nailed her squarely in the

chest. Common sense told her she was in way over her head. She gave herself a minute to fight the powerful emotions, then swallowed hard and drew in an unsteady breath. Bracing herself for the bereft feeling, she started to pull away. "Sean, I—"

He pulled her back, tightening his arms around her. "Not a chance," he said, his tone gruff. Grasping her jaw, he lifted her face, covering her mouth with a soft, sweet kiss, one that made her pulse go berserk. Her heart was pounding so hard when he finally drew away that she felt it from her scalp to her toes. He combed her hair back from her face, and then nestled her head firmly against his shoulder.

Sean gave her a tight hug, and then began rubbing her back. "Don't have second thoughts," he said quietly.

Lana pressed her face against the soft skin of his neck, her whole body trembling. She grasped the back of his head holding on to him with what little strength she had. She took a deep, shaky breath, struggling to bring things back into focus.

He smoothed his hand up her back, his jaw pressed tightly against her temple. "Just so you know," he said, as if warning her, "I never throw in a poker hand, Dempsey." He carefully tucked some of her wet hair behind her ear, his touch oddly comforting. When he spoke again, there was a touch of amusement in his voice. "And I sure as hell don't quit while I'm ahead."

That prompted a shaky laugh, and the tension abruptly drained out of her. "I didn't take you for a gambler, O'Neil."

"Shows you that you don't know everything about me." He wrapped his wet towel around his waist. "You'd better exit first."

Still stunned by what she had done, she dazedly turned and started to leave, her knees threatening to buckle with every step.

No, she didn't know everything about him. She didn't know how sexy his voice sounded when he was aroused or the way he would feel against her, his penis thick and hard. She hadn't known those things. What she'd known about Sean was his ability to always understand how she felt. How he supported his family to the point of having no life of his own. A man who *gave* in every sense of the word. She wondered what would happen if Sean suddenly decided he wanted to take. She shivered with the thought of his dormant power. A power, if unleashed, would be purely devastating. And everyone, including her, would have to watch out.

She felt as if she'd been run over by a Mack truck.

3

"HEY, BRO?"

Sean looked up as his eighteen-year-old brother came across the garage floor of the fire station. Where Sean was tall and muscular, Riley was shorter and skinnier, but with a promise of a robust male body that he only had to grow into. His hair was longer and more blond, his eyes blue. He was wearing a pair of surfer shorts and a white muscle T-shirt.

"Riley, what are you doing here?" Sean set down his overnight bag.

Lana walked by and tousled Riley's hair.

"Hi, Lana."

"Hi yourself."

"I came to ask you to do me a favor," Riley said, running his hand nervously through his hair.

"Again?"

"Isn't that like the second time this week. But who's counting."

"I'm supposed to mow the lawn, but Jeff called and said the waves are radical right now."

Sean's gaze flashed to his brother's expensive

surfboard tacked down to his car roof. His brother turned to look.

Sean's eyebrows rose and his eyes narrowed. "I guess you were pretty sure of yourself."

Lana chuckled and called, "Good luck, Sean." Her eyes lingered on his face. He watched as she disappeared around the side of the doorway.

His brother snapped his fingers in Sean's face to get his attention. "You always help me out, man."

"Shirking your chores to go to the beach to surf is irresponsible, Riley."

"I know. Just this once? I'll make it up to you. I promise."

Sean smiled. Riley was a good kid, just wave crazy. "All right. I'll do it, but you'll owe me. The next time we have a family gathering, you can go pick up Grandma."

"Sean, she always pinches my cheeks like I'm some kinda baby."

"That's the deal. Take it or leave it."

"I'll take it," he said over his shoulder as he ran for his car and jumped in. He pulled away from the curb with a screech.

Sean shook his head and headed for his car. The same old story. Good ol' Sean will always pick up the slack.

IN HER CAR, LANA THOUGHT about Sean and his family. They relied heavily on him as the oldest and

Sean never said no. Even when Lana thought they were asking too much, he just shrugged and smiled. She had to accept that it was just Sean's easygoing nature that allowed him to tolerate his family's demands.

It was three-fifteen and she was revved from turning in early last night and getting ten hours of alarm free sleep.

The first thing she did was go back to the site of the fire. She took a plastic bag with her and filled it with a sample of the soil. Afterward, she went over to the San Diego University football field and started to run the bleachers, something she did regularly. She needed a way to blow off some steam and stop herself from acting like a stupid high-schooler with a crush.

Lana had just finished when she saw a small figure way down at the bottom. She sprinted down as the figure sprinted up. Halfway, Lana saw that it was Sienna Parker, one of her women-who-dare girlfriends.

"Hey, I called the station, but they said you'd left," Sienna said when she got within hearing distance. Sienna looked radiant. Matching wits with the SEAL must really be good for her.

"And you guessed I was here," Lana replied.

"I heard about the apartment fire and your run-in with Bryant."

Lana sat down on the closest bleacher and Sienna

sat next to her. "Oh, and how did you hear about that?"

"Sean answered the phone. He told me you were edgy. I know what happens when you're edgy. You either go to Mahoney's and play a game of pool or come here."

Lana shifted on the bench. She hated to be predictable. "You checked Mahoney's?"

"Sure did. Why are you edgy?" Sienna handed Lana one of the bottles of water she was carrying. She gave Lana a rueful smile before she opened hers and took a sip.

Sweating profusely, Lana stared at the liquid in the bottle for a minute, then opened the top and took a long drink. "I'm surprised that you didn't get that information from Sean, too," she quipped.

"You *are* edgy." Sienna bumped her with her shoulder. "Still no luck with Sean?"

"I seduced him in the shower after the fire." It sounded so mild and uneventful when she said it that way, when it was anything but.

"No wonder you're out here then. After my first time with A.J., I could have jumped to the moon."

"It was incredible," Lana said.

Sienna looked at her and smiled. "You've had a crush on him for as long as I've known you. It's good to hear that it was everything you wanted it to be."

Lana took another drink, feeling pleasantly jazzed

from her run. "I have to say that it was hard to work with him after that. I wanted to find a quiet place and kiss him."

Sienna shook her head and took a drink from her own bottle. "I hear you. It was hard to keep my hands off A.J. when we were working, but I kept thinking be a professional. Must be hard for him, too. Surely you must know how much he adores you."

"What?"

Sienna rolled her eyes. "Lana, I can see it every time he looks at you."

"It was a wonderful experience and I wouldn't trade it for anything, so I'm glad he adores me. So, what's up with Kate? Has she had any luck with St. James?" Lana asked.

"No, but it hasn't been for lack of trying. I say we bring out the big guns and do her a makeover." Sienna pulled out her cell phone and dialed. "Hi, Kate. Can you get off work early?" She paused for Kate's answer then said, "Good. How about Lana and I pick you up in about an hour and we'll grab a chili dog downtown and then shop until we drop." Another pause. "That's right. It's time to make St. James sit up and beg." Lana could hear the squealing on the other end of the phone when Sienna drew it away from her ear.

Sienna and Lana grinned at each other. Sienna

flipped the phone closed. Lana said, "I'll race you. First one to the bottom gets a free chili dog."

Lana made it to the bottom first and jumped around like she'd won the New York Marathon, yelling she was number one.

As they walked to their cars, Sienna said, "I'm glad you had a good time with Sean. I'll meet you at Kate's apartment in an hour."

Lana gave her a thumbs-up and went to her house to shower. Well, actually, it was technically a bungalow that Lana had inherited from her maternal grandmother.

Her house was in great disarray because she was in the process of remodeling the whole structure while maintaining some of the old architecture, like the original leaded windows. She was proud of the finished wraparound porch that adhered to 1920 standards.

Lana went into her room and changed into a denim skirt and a SDFD T-shirt. Back in her car she drove to Kate's downtown apartment. When she got there, Sienna pulled up. Lana got out of her car and approached her friend, just as Kate emerged from her apartment to the sidewalk. After a few moments of debating who was going to drive, Sienna volunteered and they piled into her car to drive the few miles downtown.

They parked and got out, making their way through the end of the day crowds to their favorite hot dog stand. After getting the dogs, they strolled toward the trendy shops, glancing in the windows, hoping that something caught their eye.

Kate sighed, picking at the cheese on her over-stuffed hot dog. "So, it sounds like you had a really good time with Sean. The fire station showers. I don't think I could beat that."

"After we get through with you, there's no telling where you guys will do it. On his desk," Lana said, smiling wickedly. She took a bite out of her equally overstuffed dog, feeling guilty that she'd forgotten to ask Sean for her women-who-dare souvenir. She'd have to make a point of getting one from him. Easygoing Sean would probably chuckle and hand something over without a fuss.

"Wow," Kate said fanning herself. "That's a powerful fantasy. Don't give me ideas." Kate rolled her eyes. "Except the man is always on the move and hard to pin down. I don't think he knows I'm alive. He only grunts when I hand him a file as if he's too busy to lift his head. Do you think he's angry at me for the DNA case he thinks I botched?"

"Jericho strikes me as the kind of man who gets even, not angry," Lana said ruefully.

"That's a comforting thought, Lana. Thank you."

"All I'm saying is that if Jericho wants something, he goes after it. The man is intense city. I'd have him in a headlock after a few minutes of working with him."

"He's also handsome as sin, muscled to perfection, and smells heavenly," Kate said dreamily.

"You need to make your move, Kate," Sienna suggested, polishing off her dog.

"Tell me about it," Kate said.

Lana stopped in front of a boutique. "How about this little red number. *Va-va-voom*. It should get St. James's engine running."

"Why don't you try it on, Kate," Sienna said as she and Lana grabbed Kate's arm and dragged her inside the shop.

They found Kate's size and after trying on the dress Kate came out of the dressing room.

"Yowza. You'll knock his socks off, Kate. You look great in that," Lana said, admiring the scooped neckline and the wraparound style. Kate had such a perfect little body, but she hid it under conservative clothes and her white lab coat.

"I don't know. Do you think it might be too much for court?" Kate said, looking at herself in the full-length mirror, turning to get a view of the back.

"No. It's beautiful and would be perfect for court," Sienna said. "I'd wear it. It commands attention and looks professional, too."

"It's expensive," Kate stated, looking at the price tag.

"It's worth it. I'd love to see St. James's face when he sees you in that," Sienna said.

"You're getting it," Lana said. "When's your next court date?"

"Next week."

"Good." Lana walked up to her and put her hands on her shoulders. "Now the next thing to go is your glasses. How do you feel about contact lenses?"

"Actually I've already scheduled laser surgery, so that I don't need corrective lenses at all."

Lana looked at Sienna and they grinned at each other. "Now the hair," Sienna said as she undid the pins that held Kate's hair in a tight bun. It cascaded all the way past her butt.

"He doesn't stand a chance," Lana said, turning her very attractive friend back toward the full-length mirror. "You'll have him at your mercy in no time."

AFTER HER SHOPPING EXCURSION, Lana gave Kate the evidence bag and asked her to analyze the soil inside for accelerants. Before heading home, Lana stopped at the store and picked up milk, eggs and a few other staples. Back in the car, she drove to her father's house.

Her father was a former San Diego firefighter who had been disabled twenty years ago when he'd fallen through a floor and messed up his knee. Unable to continue as a firefighter, he'd gone on permanent disability. The injury cut his career short and ended a three-generation tradition of Dempsey men who'd become captain.

But as Lana was told over and over again by her grandfather and father, she would redeem that time-honored tradition and restore the family's pride. She had had to. When her brother decided that he wanted to be a park ranger after he saw the public service announcements for Smokey the Bear, Lana was the one her father turned to since her brother had lost interest in firefighting at a young age.

Lana parked her car in the driveway, admiring the beautiful array of flowers that she'd planted for him two weeks ago. It looked like he was keeping up with the watering.

She didn't bother to knock as she opened the front door and made her way to the kitchen.

"Lana? That you?"

Lana set the groceries on the counter and started to unpack the bag. "I brought you a few things," she yelled.

He ambled into the kitchen and leaned against the doorjamb. "You didn't have to do that, you know. I'm mobile."

Working at keeping her patience, she said, "I know you are, Dad. I was at the store and I know you don't always keep track of what's in the fridge."

He folded his arms across his chest and gave her a wry look. Clearing his throat, he asked, "So, are you all set for the lieutenant's exam?"

"Dad, do we have to talk about the damn exam again? I'm ready to take it." This time she couldn't keep the emotion out of her voice. Although she'd wanted to become captain since she was a little girl, recently she'd been on edge about the exam and not sure why.

"There's no need to curse, Lana. You know how much this means to your grandfather and to me. We're very proud of you. The eighty-second has had a Dempsey heading it up since the fire department's inception. They need smart women like you in a leadership position. You have the potential to achieve a pinnacle that was denied me. Your mother, God rest her soul, would be so proud of you."

She closed her eyes, praying for more patience to deal with her father. "I appreciate your confidence in my abilities. Now, did you eat today?"

AFTER PREPARING HER FATHER a good meal of steak, potatoes and a salad, they had a pleasant time talking about her sister Paige, who was doing very well in her business and would be marrying FBI agent Justin Connor next year. Her brother Alex excelled as a Park Ranger at a Northern California park and had just been in the paper recently for saving a kay-aker on the river.

When she left his house, she was feeling restless. She decided to head over to Mahoney's for a quick beer and some conversation. She could always depend on some of her friends being there.

She couldn't regret what she'd shared with Sean. Never that. She knew that she wanted him from the moment she'd laid eyes on him, but did he feel the same?

MAHONEY'S WAS THE PLACE people went to get away from everyday stress. Although food was served, it was a bar and didn't try to hide it. Sean loved the atmosphere where yuppies mingled with leather-clad bikers and pierced punkers.

Although busy and crowded, the noise didn't affect Sean. He was too busy thinking about Lana Dempsey.

It had been much easier on Sean when he could pretend that Lana was nothing more than a friend. He'd hung out with her, drank with her, played pool with her and worked with her. Now, after that steamy time in the shower he couldn't stop thinking about her. He realized that he'd never stopped thinking about her since he'd first met her.

He'd just been kidding himself.

In denial.

In fact, he'd never admit this to her, but he had protective instincts where she was concerned. When they had first started working together, he'd watched out for her, but it was soon evident that Lana did her job and did it well. In addition to having the hots for her, she was one hell of a good firefighter.

She was also one hell of a good friend, he reminded himself again. In fact, if it hadn't been for her, he didn't think he'd be a firefighter today.

Oh, he hadn't had a problem with attending lectures or the fire scene simulations. The couple and uncoupling of hoses, naming extinguishers and their specific uses was a piece of cake. He excelled with the learning and use of the Chicago door opener and the ten-pound maul.

But the word *ladder* made him break out in a cold sweat. He'd never admitted it to her in the six years they'd been friends, but he was afraid of heights. Not in a paralyzing way, but enough that it caused him difficulty in some maneuvers for his job.

There was no such thing as mundane as a ladder in the fire department. There were two-person ladders, hydraulic ladders and even a three-hundred-and-fifty-pound ladder that required six people to lift and place. At least all these ladders afforded him hand and footholds and the semblance of safety.

Not the case with a pompier. Deemed too dangerous for use in everyday firefighting, the brass didn't bat an eyelash when it came to ordering recruits to climb the fourteen-foot-long pieces of wood with small handles that ran up either side of the dinosaurlike vertebrae to test their mettle.

The first day they were introduced to the pompier, he'd had a panic attack. Yet, regardless of the fear, Sean was determined he would get through the maneuvers. He remembered Lana and he stood side-by-side to begin the exercise. They were to flip the top of the pompier to the sill of the window above and when it caught, they had to climb.

The muscling of the pompier into place against a seven-story building wasn't a problem for him, but when he looked way up, he felt his stomach flip. It was then that Lana turned to him and said, "I'll race you."

The fierce competitive look on her face gave him the momentum to grab the handles and begin to climb, but he wasn't prepared for the way the threadlike frame bent and swayed.

He'd felt bile rise when he heard the creak and groan of the windowsill above, the only thing that held him aloft. But it was only the beginning.

At the sixth window, their trainer yelled, "Belt yourself to the ladder."

With slick hands, he did as he was told, but he froze when the command came.

"Lean back."

Sean knew he was going to lose it right then and

there, but he'd glanced over at Lana. She was leaning out with her arms wide as if she was on a cross. She had a rapturous look on her face as if it was the most wonderful experience in the world.

He swallowed his fear and leaned slowly away from the safety of the building, feeling as if any moment the earth would rush up to greet him. Sweating and cursing under his breath, he opened his arms and hung there suspended with his eyes closed, keeping that image of Lana's face in his mind until they were told to come back down.

He thought about going over to her house. He loved Lana's house from the light green paint he'd help put on the new siding to the porch she'd lovingly restored. But he especially loved the riot of flowers that gave the bungalow an English garden feel to it. It would be a nice place to come home to.

Sean lived in a boring apartment on the twenty-third floor. It had a great view, but definitely lacked the cozy feeling of Lana's place.

He had no doubt she would open the door with a smile and a greeting.

So why were his palms sweaty and his heart pounding as he thought about walking up to her bungalow to drop in on her unannounced?

The unexpected sight of her sidling up to the bar and ordering a beer made him forget all about flowers, porches and paint. Sean marveled how she was able to take his breath away. Even with soot on her face, helmet hair and the scent of smoke about her, she looked beautiful to him.

He got up from the table he was sitting at and made his way over to the bar.

"Hey," he said by way of greeting.

When he tried to look in her eyes, she was turning away to grab her purse to pay for the beer. For a moment, he wondered if she was shy around him now that they'd been intimate or was she as confused about how to act around him as he was about how to act around her.

He covered her hand as she pulled out her wallet. "I got it, Lana."

She looked up at him and down at his hand, her eyes telling him that she liked his touch. His doubts dissipated along with the fear that had settled in his abdomen.

"Thanks, O'Neill. Did you get the lawn mowed?"

"No, I have to run into town tomorrow and replace the mower blade. You'd think that Riley would notice the thing's rusted."

"If you made him take responsibility instead of always saying yes to his demands, he might."

Sean shifted, knowing she was right, but in the past doing favors for his family hadn't been a big deal.

Lana eyed him and continued, "But Riley's surf

crazy and you know it. He's good, Sean. Has he thought about going pro?''

"Don't encourage him. That's all he ever talks about.''

Lana took a sip of her beer and Sean studied her face. "Where have you been? You're glowing with that smug look that tells me you've been up to no good.''

Lana flashed him a wicked grin. "I have been. Sienna, Kate and I were on a mission of utmost importance.''

"That sounds ominous. What are you three up to?''

"Oh, only a shopping excursion to buy something to snag a special man Kate is trying to entice.''

"Who's the poor sap?''

"Jericho St. James.''

"The prosecutor and Kate? Mmm. St. James is too intense.''

"Are you saying that Kate can't handle him?''

"She's so sweet. If he hurt her, I'd hate to get arrested for punching out the prosecutor.''

"Oh, Sean. Always the big brother.''

"Not always," he said softly close to her ear. He smiled when he felt her tremble.

She took a big breath. "So what do you say about another beer and a game of pool?''

"Sounds good. I'll get the beer, you go rack up a table.''

He was relieved that their relationship seemed as easy and effortless as always.

They took a table near the back of the bar. Sean was hoping that no one from the station would come in. He selfishly wanted the time with Lana.

Lana had already racked up the balls and he set the beer down at a nearby table.

"Want me to break?" she asked, picking up her mug and taking a swallow.

"Sure go ahead."

Lana was a good pool player, and although he was a better player, he always let her win.

The break scattered the balls across the table. She called her first shot. "Nine ball in the corner pocket."

Sean watched as she did a good job. When it was his turn, he took two shots and botched the third.

She smiled and slapped him on the bottom as she passed. Caught off guard, he turned to look at her.

"What's the matter, O'Neill?"

"Keep it up, Dempsey."

She stuck her tongue out at him. "I will."

They played until the last of the solid balls were gone. She did a good job of beating him. He didn't much care about that. He just liked being with her. Then she sank the eight ball with a pretty impressive shot.

He came up to her and gave her a high-five. "You've been practicing."

"I have to, O'Neill, so you'll stop letting me win."

"I don't…" She tickled him in the ribs and he jumped back.

"Yes, you do, you sweet liar."

When she sat down, she crossed her legs and his eyes riveted to her well-defined calves in the short skirt she wore. The skirt hugged every curve of her sexy body. Even the routine SDFD T-shirt she wore looked sexy on her. He couldn't help wondering what she was wearing under her clothes.

"I'll get us more beer and some pretzels," he said as he headed for the bar. Tim Mahoney manned the bar, a fellow Irishman who had come from Ireland and opened up this establishment.

A soccer game played on the television above the bar. The walls decorated with Irish trappings.

Sean held up his fingers to indicate two beers and Tim filled two glasses and slid them over the bar into Sean's waiting hands. He grabbed a bowl of pretzels and headed back to the table.

When he got there, Lana sat talking with two squad members from the station, Pete Meadows and Ron Sharp. Pete was a womanizer and Ron was a natural born charmer. They had both mentioned to him how hot Lana was. A possessive feeling that was new to him served to increase his pace. He put down the beers and pretzels. He, Ron and Pete exchanged greetings.

Sean spent the rest of the evening vying for Lana's attention and playing a tug of war with Pete over buying her beers. A couple of times she gave him a sharp look as if to say, "What is wrong with you?" But he was in agony watching Lana flirt with Pete and Ron. Finally, as other people they knew filtered back to their table, Sean had had enough and rose.

"Lana, I'll walk you out."

She was busy greeting a cop friend of Sienna's, Rosa Santana. "I'm not ready to leave yet," she said, frowning. She looked at her watch. "It's still early."

At that moment, the band started to play and Pete rose, "Lana would you like to dance?"

"She's dancing with me," Sean said and put his hand on her wrist.

"I thought you were leaving, O'Neill," Pete said, taking her other wrist.

"Could you both stop." She shook off their hands. "I don't feel like dancing right now," Lana said testily, giving Sean a narrowed-eyed look that could melt steel.

For the rest of the evening he fumed, but acted like his easygoing self. He didn't want his friends and squad members to catch onto the fact that his and Lana's relationship had changed.

But it hadn't really. They were still friends, right? Sex was the only thing that had really changed in their relationship. When Lana finally got up to go, Sean said he was leaving, too.

They got into their separate cars and she waved to him as she pulled out of the parking lot. He beeped his horn and headed in the other direction toward his apartment. But the more he thought about Pete and Ron, the more he wanted to define his sexual relationship with Lana.

He turned his car around and headed for Lana's house. When he got to Lana's bungalow, she was just getting out of her car.

Before he could even get out of the car, Lana said through his open window, "If you've come to apologize, I'm not in the mood. That was very subtle, Sean. I don't particularly like to be used in a tug of war."

Sean sat there and watched her quick steps up the walk and cursed to himself.

With more force then necessary, he opened the door and slammed it closed. He marched up to her house while she was still fumbling with the lock.

He said through clenched teeth, "I didn't like the way Pete was looking at you."

"What do you have to say about it? We're friends." She tried harder to get the door open, not even glancing at him.

"As a friend, I'm giving you advice. He's a womanizer."

"Don't you think I know that? I'm not stupid."

She jiggled the lock, the nervous trembling of her hands making the simple turning of a key into a major chore. When he suddenly leaned into her to help her with the door, the shock of sensation that coursed through him left him weak and shaking.

"Will you stop it," she cried loudly, as he tried to help her with the door. She turned around and he wobbled into her. The door unexpectedly opened and since he was leaning so heavily against her, she completely lost her balance and the both of them went sprawling onto the hardwood floor.

She gasped as he landed on top of her. She pushed ineffectually at him as she spat out, "Get off me, you idiot. You're crushing me." She wheezed, unable to keep the laughter out of her voice.

He'd never had a fight with Lana before, mostly because he was so laid back. Add sex to the mix and this is what happened. He was jealous. His father always told him to just apologize to a woman. No matter whether you thought you were right or not. Lana was too important to him to fight with her.

Sean braced his arms on either side of her head and lifted himself off, so that she could finally inhale. He looked at her, her eyes shining. Warm amusement sent a wry smile to his lips and he was chuckling, and then laughing.

Between bursts he forced out, "I'm sorry. I've been a complete jerk," he continued more calmly.

They both burst out laughing again, and Lana

choked out, "Yes, you were. Whatever possessed you to one up him like that all night? I've never seen you like that, Sean."

The laughter faded from his face and he smiled at her, a lazy contented smile. He shifted and the door slammed.

"Seems like you bring out the best and the worst in me," he said as he lifted his hand and gently touched her mouth. "Such beautiful lips." Sean suppressed a groan of desire.

He tensed, coiled like a spring. His whole being centered on the soft skin of her mouth beneath his caressing fingers.

A primeval passion was slowly building between them, erupting and completely eclipsing all other thoughts and emotions.

He knew then that their relationship wouldn't ever go back to what it had been. No more simple dinners and platonic camping trips. No more friendly late-night conversations that lasted into the morning. Instead he'd want to be in her bed until morning.

He closed his eyes against the yearning. Damn, how he needed her, how he craved her, wanting to make her part of him. The memory of the feel of her wet body pressing against his in the shower filled his mind. He lowered his head, seeking and finding her sweet mouth. At the touch of Lana's tongue against his, Sean groaned deeply, his fingers tightening in the tangled chestnut hair as he hungrily took the kiss she so feverishly offered him. "You taste so good. You feel so good. I want you so damn much, I'm going out of my mind."

"Shut up and kiss me. I want your mouth. I want you. *How I want you.*"

Her words consumed him with desire. He ached to drive into her moist, enchanting flesh that so tortured and yet aroused him beyond thought. An elemental force gripped him. Her fevered squirming was a fiery torture, her compliance, a carnal stimulus. Her response dissolved that thin facade of humanity and roused the elemental urge to conquer her. He pushed himself away from her, kneeling over her, his hands going to the hem of the cotton shirt. He stripped it from her body and she moaned softly.

He couldn't even make the transition from the floor to the bedroom or stop his frantic movements to remove her clothing, longing to feel her naked flesh against him. He got rid of their clothing, fully covering her lithe body with his. He could feel the heat of her all along his hot skin, feel hard points of her sensitive nipples against the smooth expanse of his chest, feel her erratic breathing and her hammering heart.

His mouth left hers and his thumb brushed over her mouth. His open palm cupped her face, the soft caress of his fingertips running down her neck, over her breasts, tantalizing the soft nipples into stiff rosy peaks.

With a low growl of satisfaction, his mouth closed over first one then the other, his teeth grazing the hardened peaks with an acute ache that drew an intense moan of frustrated desire from deep in his chest.

He had never felt such intense desire. She arched her back in response to the delicious sensation of his moist tongue swirling around and licking the tips of her breasts.

With the heel of his hand, he pressed against her sensitive skin, stoking the fires that burned within her to a white-hot heat. Feeling the wetness of her desire against his skin, he pushed rhythmically upward again and again. His breath caught with each sugared moan, and her hips arched sensuously against his hand, pushing herself against him wantonly.

Sean's tenuous restraint fractured and broke, the fears becoming meaningless to him as if it were nothing but nonsensical gibberish. His mouth moved down to the soft flesh of her stomach, kissing her and brushing his lips along her soft skin, seeking her inviting wetness.

His hands gripped the waistband of the panties she wore and he slowly removed them as his mouth trailed along the exposed skin. The only barrier left between them.

He spread her slender thighs, his head dipping down to the warm honeyed mound and with his tongue he found the very center of her desire. He stroked upward, breathing in the hot tang of her arousal. Lana thrashed and twisted beneath him, moaning in heightened ecstasy, gasping as she came apart in his arms.

He surged up the length of her body and his words were heartfelt and simple. "I was jealous and I'm sorry."

She cupped his face between her hands and kissed his mouth.

He rooted around in his jeans and used the protection he found there. With a low growl of satisfaction, his own ravenous needs would no longer be denied. Without missing a beat, he buried the painful, burning shaft of his desire full-length into her moist sheath.

He jerked in wondered sensual amazement, moaning uncontrollably as the ache spread inside him and he thrust harder into her.

She eagerly accepted his deep thrusts into her body. She writhed beneath him as he lost himself in the red haze of wild desire, eager to reach that exquisite peak of pleasure she had just enjoyed. Her hands reached up, gripping the shiny mass of his hair, dragging his head down to her waiting lips. Her legs locked around his lean driving hips, her body meeting and joining with the rhythmic movements of his. He filled her, fully meeting each drive with a provocative thrust of her hips. His mind went blank as he felt the tiny warning tremors heralding the powerful attainment of his fulfillment.

Sean was lost in a sea of pent-up burning desire. He thrust into her mindlessly. The feel of her lips sent detonations of pleasure exploding along his heightened nerve endings. He ravaged her mouth, biting her lips, sliding his tongue along her moist sensitive flesh. This wasn't a figment of his fevered imagination; her beautiful face was inches from his, flushed with desire, her shining hair spread over the hardwood floor like liquid sable.

He wanted to continue to do this all night, moving steadily and slowly inside her, but she slid her fingers through his hair at his nape, clutching them tightly and tugging and lifting her hips, whispering, "Sean, please."

The exquisite sweetness of his name on her lips and the tantalizing movement of her body responding to his tore a profound groan from him. He drove into her, thrusting again and again, plunging his tongue into her welcoming mouth and, at that moment, she jerked against him with deep rhythmic spasms. Spasms that forced a wrenching groan out of her. Sean moaned softly as he stopped thrusting in response to wave after wave of intense pleasure that tore through him. He convulsed in wild ecstasy and they exploded together into mutual rapture.

He collapsed against her, his skin hot and moist, his breathing labored. He moved to his side to keep from crushing her. Taking her with him, he curled his arm around her back, his fingers buried in her hair. He pulled her up with him quickly.

With a gentle tug of her hand, she led him through the darkened house to her bedroom. She pulled him down onto the softness of the mattress, holding him close to her. He felt light as air, as light as a feather. His hand drifted lazily down her body and up again to tangle in her hair.

He felt her kiss his neck and brush her lips along his collar bone before she whispered against his ear, sending shivers of delight playing over his skin, ''Apology accepted.''

He tightened his hold on her and sighed in relief, allowing the delicious feel of her to lull him into sleep.

4

SEAN WOKE TO THE SOUND of the shower, momentarily confused. He opened his eyes, his gaze roving around the room. The rosebud border he'd helped to install a month ago made his brow knit. He sat bolt upright in bed. Her bed. He'd spent the night in Lana's bed.

He rubbed his hand over his face and into his hair. This shouldn't be so strange. After all he was very close to her, nonetheless pretending this whole thing didn't unnerve him wouldn't help.

Was she as confused as he was?

Probably not. Women always seemed to know in what direction they wanted to go. At least Lana always seemed confident and in control of most situations. He really liked that about her.

The water went off. He swung his feet to the floor. He slipped out of her room and gathered up the clothes he'd left in the foyer. Quickly he dressed and went into her kitchen. The least he could do was cook her some breakfast.

He started the coffee. It looked like she'd been shopping yesterday. She had more in the fridge than he did. He took out eggs and bacon and put six strips of bacon in a pan. He cracked the eggs and automatically made them sunny side up. They both liked them the same way. He knew that because he'd cooked for her numerous times at the station house.

He thought about how easygoing it had always been with Lana from the moment a woman had invaded the all man station. They'd had some hardcore firefighters who believed that women didn't belong, but Lana soon won them over with her open personality and her awesome abilities.

When he looked up from putting bread in the toaster she was standing in the doorway.

"Smells good."

He froze like an idiot when he saw her. He'd never seen Lana through the eyes of a man who'd just emerged from her bed.

She stood there looking at him, eyes wide and dark, lips moist and slightly parted. She wasn't doing a damn thing and still she managed to exude sexuality. Her hair was in its usual tamed state, shiny brown and damp from her shower. She wore a temptation red T-shirt, veed at the neckline to expose her creamy throat and just a hint of cleavage that made Sean's fingers itch to trace her skin. Faded and snug jeans tapered to low-slung Western cut booties. A tooled leather belt snugged her waist.

She dropped her eyes, looking unsure of herself, vulnerable. The desire to gather her in his arms and protect her hit Sean so hard that it damn near knocked the wind out of him. He turned away and cleared his throat, pushing the lever on the toaster to drop the toast down.

Lana wouldn't appreciate the fact that he wanted to protect her. But he couldn't help it.

He realized he hadn't spoken to her. It was probably the reason she was so nervous. He said, "It's almost ready."

"Good. I'm starved."

She came over and went to the fridge. As she passed, he could smell the scent of raspberries in her freshly washed hair, the delicious fragrance of her warm body. She took margarine out of the fridge and closed the door. Opening the drawer near her hip, she pulled out a knife and bumped it closed with a flick of her hip.

He dropped the spatula on the floor.

Lana stilled, her eyes going to the utensil lying on the floor, and then up to his face.

Sean rubbed the back of his neck and met her eyes, his heart beating hard in his chest.

"The eggs are burning," Lana said softly.

Swiftly Sean pulled the pan from the flame. Sheepishly he picked up the spatula and put it in the sink.

"You don't have to stay or make me breakfast. You don't have to feel guilty, Sean."

He heard the irritation in her voice and turned to

face her. Drawing in a deep breath, he said, "I know that. I just don't know how to handle…"

"Me?" She shot him a disgruntled look.

"This thing between us."

"Lust?"

"It's more than that and you know it. I'm a clear-cut guy. Women usually fall into two categories. Friends or lovers. I don't mix the two and I find it extremely irritating that I've found both in you."

Lana shrugged and sat down at her little round table. He liked everything about her kitchen, the homey feel and the soft feminine lace curtains on the window overlooking the beautiful view of her English garden. The choice of sunny yellow on the walls with the rich wood of the floor was a comforting combination. He just felt so much at… well…at home.

That feeling and his emotions for Lana were all twisted up inside him.

"We have chemistry and we gave in to our needs. Are you saying that you can't get past that?" she asked quietly.

Sean had that same ugly sensation that their relationship was changing too much for him to keep up with it. He just plain didn't know how to respond to her.

"No. The sex was great. You're great. I just don't want to lose our friendship." It sounded lame even to his ears, but her eyes softened as he finished.

"We won't."

"It's already changed." His voice was very quiet, very serious.

"Relationships change, Sean. You either move with them or leave them behind."

Feeling the emotional weight of that statement, Sean moved across the floor. Damned if he would lose Lana as a friend. He grabbed her arm and pulled her up from her chair, closing in on her as if his sheer presence could make her change her mind. "Leaving our relationship behind isn't an option."

When she smiled, his heart turned over in his chest. She was such a beautiful woman.

"Good," she whispered softly.

He sighed. "Is that all you can say?"

She cupped his face. "If it's any consolation, I don't want to lose our friendship either. Can't we just agree that we're friends and leave it at that?"

"Friends who sleep together," he clarified.

"What's wrong with that?"

He sighed again. "Nothing, I guess, as long as sex doesn't…"

She put her fingers over his lips. "Sean, you think way too much."

He kissed her fingers. She seemed so nonchalant. Maybe that's what got to him. Maybe it didn't mean as much to her as it meant to him. It could be why she was acting like this wasn't a big deal. Friends or lovers. He didn't like it and wanted to push her, but knew that pushing Lana would net him nothing. She'd probably become angry and throw him out. Where would he be then?

"Why don't you go take a shower? I've got my arson class today."

Sean looked down at his watch. "And I've got to get the lawn mower fixed. I was supposed to be there ten minutes ago. I'd better call."

"There's a phone in my room."

When Sean left, Lana grabbed the pan off the stove and put it in the sink. She leaned against the counter and took a deep breath. Everything Sean had said had merit. But she didn't know what was going to happen and worrying about it only caused more problems. Sean was too much of a good friend to ever disappear from her life. She had to believe that.

But her gut churned with the effort it took not to show him how much he meant to her. His friendship was more important than anything else, but if they started analyzing everything it could only end in disaster.

Sean came back after twenty minutes, his hair wet. He gave her a rough kiss and drove off.

She didn't know what she was going to do with him, but she thought it might be fun to find out. Sex brought them one step closer to a more intimate relationship. She'd always shared her thoughts and time with Sean. Now sharing her body seemed so natural.

It had been wonderful to wake up to him this morning. His face seemed so peaceful in sleep. She'd watched his serene, sleeping face for long moments before she'd gotten into the shower. If it hadn't been for her class, she would have stayed in bed with him all day.

Her first stop was to the SDPD labs and Kate. When she got out of the car, she saw Bryant talking to Sienna near the entrance. She'd have to pump Sienna for information on that as soon as she was done with Kate.

She went around to the side door and down the stairs. At the bottom, she turned right and went through a gray metal door. Kate was loading a slide when Lana walked into her lab.

"Hey," Kate said, giving Lana a big smile. "What brings you here so early on this beautiful morning? Isn't it your day off?"

Lana got right to the point. The other thing on her mind, besides Sean, had been the soil sample and if it contained remnants of the accelerant she was sure would be there. "The soil. Did you have time to analyze it?"

"Right. I should have guessed. Dane the pain was just in here."

"Did he request a soil test, too?" Lana asked as she sat down on one of the stools close to the counter.

"No. He gave me some charred wood to analyze

on a different case,'' she said walking into her office and searching through a stack of papers on her desk.

"He refuses to believe that there's a killer out there. I'm going to prove him wrong. This guy deliberately set fires on the fourth floor and the basement. It was designed to trap the residents inside."

"What evidence do you have to support that?" Kate asked.

"The spalling in the basement. I'm sure a fire was set there."

"Spalling usually occurs when there's an intense fire. Didn't the lobby collapse from above?"

"Yes," Lana said.

"Couldn't it have caused fire in the basement?"

"No. Because if a fire was set in the fourth floor apartment how could it have gotten to the lobby?"

"It traveled."

"Nope. Fire never descends. It always travels up. That's the science of fire, but you knew that. You were testing me."

Kate smiled. "Just seeing if you were on your toes."

Kate pulled out her report. "You're right. There was evidence of accelerant in the soil."

"I knew it. I'm going back to the first suspicious fire and gather another sample. You willing to analyze that one, too?"

"Unofficially?"

Lana rolled her eyes. "Yes, since I have no authority to be doing this."

Kate laughed. "I broke the rules for you when Paige was in trouble with that FBI agent. What makes you think I would ever let you down, Lana?"

"I know you're already in hot water with St. James."

It was Kate's turn to roll her eyes. "I can handle him."

"I have no doubts about that."

"After you left us yesterday, did you see Sean?"

Excitement at the mention of Sean's name washed into her system. "I went to Mahoney's and he followed me home," Lana said, suddenly breathless. "This morning he was torn between the lovers and friends thing."

Kate looked worried. "And that doesn't bother you?"

"Why should it?" Lana shrugged. "I know that Sean will always be in my life."

"Do you want more from this, Lana?"

"I don't know. My path is already set for me. My career is high priority. Making captain is all I've worked for and I can't let anything jeopardize that."

Kate touched Lana's arm. "Sometimes I think that you repress so much it comes as second nature to you."

Lana viewed Kate thoughtfully for a moment. "What do you mean?"

"Lana, I know you're crazy about Sean, but you act like it's no big deal. Deep inside I'm sure you're in as much turmoil as he is, but God forbid anyone should know about it. You don't have to hide your real feelings all the time."

They walked back out to Kate's lab. Lana said, "I'm just trying to keep everything in perspective. And I'm not repressing anything. Sean and I are friends first. Once we get this sex thing out of our system, things will go back to normal."

"You keep telling yourself that, Lana and you might believe it."

She gave Kate a cheeky grin, knowing that she was safe in her belief. She leaned over and looked into the microscope. "Looks like a match."

"Sorry you didn't go into forensic science instead of firefighting?"

Lana raised her head. "Once a geek, always a geek I guess. I love this stuff, but it doesn't compare to firefighting. Even though I majored in fire science in college, I minored in chemistry."

"Why anyone would want to take organic chemistry when they didn't have to is beyond me."

"You aced that class, Kate."

"I know, but it doesn't mean I love it. Now the science of DNA, that's a different story."

Lana looked at her watch. "I've got to go or I'll be late."

Kate handed Lana the report and said, "Be careful. Dane will be livid when he finds out what you're doing. Call me if you need anything else.''

Lana gave Kate a hug. ''You're the best.''

Lana emerged into the parking lot and came face to face with Dane Bryant.

''What are you doing here, Dempsey?''

Everything the man said had that undertone of a sneer. It immediately put Lana on edge. ''Seeing a friend.''

His eyes narrowed at her. She chafed against the restraint of his rank. She wished she could tell him to go to hell, but her training won over her pique. She'd be damned if she let him rile her enough to give him a reason to slap an insubordination charge on her. She needed her record to be impeccable. They didn't choose captains from hotheads and troublemakers.

Although this clandestine investigation could be considered troublemaking, but only if she got caught before she found the bad guy. Bryant, with all his posturing and bravado, wasn't any closer to solving the arson than he was three weeks ago.

Bryant sneered at her, ''Stay out of my way.'' He pushed past her and Lana watched him go. He might have been an excellent firefighter, but he wasn't a very good arson investigator. She wondered how he'd gotten the job.

''That guy has it in for you.''

Lana turned at the sound of Sienna's voice. "No kidding, but he doesn't intimidate me. He's a jerk."

"And I can see that you would love to tell him that to his face."

"Yep, but can't. Regulations on insubordination are pretty clear-cut."

"I know all about that."

"What were you two talking about?"

"We were discussing the arsonist that has struck two apartment houses. Dane thinks it might be an arson for hire."

"He's wrong."

Sienna raised her brow. "You know that for a fact."

"I found spalling in the basement of the second fire. Dane said that because the roof collapsed, it caused the basement fire. I say there was spalling because someone set a fire down there. I asked him to check it out by taking a sample of the soil."

"But he dismissed you, so you, in your pit-bull way, asked Kate to do a sample for you on the sly."

"Right."

"Lana, Dane would love to discredit you and get you kicked off the force. You need to be careful."

"He's incompetent. His sexism is interfering with an investigation. I can't sit by while he stumbles around in the dark and gets nowhere."

"Be careful." A gleam came into her eye. "How goes it with Sean?"

Lana gave Sienna the same report she'd given Kate and Sienna had the same reaction.

"I'll be careful. Look, I've got to go, but I'll talk to you later."

She parted with Sienna, trying to ignore the worried look on her friend's face. It was hard to believe that only a year ago, she neither knew Sienna, nor was likely to become friends with her. Then Paige got in trouble and both Kate and Sienna had come into her life. They had stood by her every step of the way and together they had formed a bond that locked them together as close as sisters.

That was why it had been so easy to challenge her friends into a souvenir-gathering escapade. After Sienna suggested that Lana was afraid of Sean sexually, Lana had insisted on a contest. Sienna had ended up going after the sexy SEAL she'd been assigned to work with and now Sienna had an engagement ring on her finger. Lana didn't have that expectation with Sean. This was just a fling for her and all this caution from her friends was overkill.

Sienna waved as Lana started up the car. She smiled and waved back. The worried look hadn't disappeared and Lana remembered all too well that Sienna had already experienced what it was like to go after a man who was a challenge. But was Sean someone who wouldn't work in her life? Where did he fit? Lover? Friend? Squad member? Or all three?

Achieving balance was always topmost on Lana's

list of things that made her feel comfortable, but Sean didn't fit into any easily defined holes, round or square.

All she knew was that he made her tingle. Her heart skipped a beat whenever she saw the familiar slope of his shoulders, that charismatic smile, or the sheen of his hair in the sun. His voice mesmerized her, a voice she could listen to for hours.

Shaking her head to clear it, Lana was aware of the pitfalls of getting involved with Sean and she'd decided he was worth the risk. But daydreaming, her father had told her, would only make her lose focus. He'd told her countless times that she had to be strong to make it in a man's profession. Letting emotion get in her way was dangerous.

Arriving ten minutes late for her class, she took her seat quickly. She tried to push Sean out of her mind, but he wouldn't go. The best she could do was to keep him at bay.

SEAN APPROACHED THE BACK DOOR. Inside he could hear his mother talking to his aunt Maggie.

"Megan, you have that son of yours constantly running around like a crazy person. I can pick up Mom's present."

"Sean's a good boy. He doesn't mind," his mother said, absolute conviction in her voice.

"Don't you think he might like to have his days off free to do something fun?" his aunt said in exasperation. "If he's not doing something for Riley or you, he's doing something for his dad."

"I told you. Sean doesn't mind," his mother replied calmly.

Sean opened the back door, making enough noise so that his mother and aunt could hear him. "Hi, Mom," he bussed his mother's cheek and turned to his aunt and gave her a kiss, too. "And you, Aunt Maggie."

"Sean, dear. I saved you some breakfast. It's on the stove. Thank you for fixing the lawn mower. We really appreciate it. You know how hard it is to get your father to do anything."

"Thanks, Mom." He walked over to the pan and lifted the lid. Eggs, hash browns and bacon were all nestled nicely together in the skillet and heated just enough to eat without getting burned. Although he'd stopped on the way and eaten, he pulled down a plate.

"Sean," his mother said, glancing at his aunt. "While you're downtown getting a new blade, could you pick up a gift for your grandmother's birthday?"

Sean doesn't mind. Those were his mother's words and the sentiment behind them was true. He didn't mind doing things for his family, but had Lana been right when she said they were taking advantage of him?

"I can do it, Mom."

His mother gave his aunt a grin and Sean forked up his food and continued eating.

IT TOOK TWO HOURS and three hardware stores before Sean finally gave up and bought his parents a new lawnmower.

He loaded the purchase in the car and spied a vintage record store one building over. He knew his grandmother loved old albums and it would be a good place to get a gift for her.

He locked his car and walked toward the store, but stopped in front of an outdoor shop sandwiched between the hardware and record stores.

In the window was a mock climbing wall along with climbing gear. Sean stood in front of the glass for a long time staring at the equipment, wondering if he could finally overcome his fear of heights. He looked at the wall and spied the notice for climbing classes. Then looked at the wall again. He really was busy taking care of his family's needs. Maybe later.

With a last look at the gear, he went into the record store.

WHEN HER CLASS WAS OVER, Lana retrieved Kate's report. She felt no satisfaction that she'd been right. It only meant that Bryant was going on wrong assumptions and poorly gathered data.

Lana felt a chill slide down her neck. This kind of deliberate act most likely would escalate. So far the SDFD had been able to save all the lives involved in the two blazes. But fire was a deadly and clever foe and eventually it could claim a life.

She couldn't let that happen. Dropping the report on the seat, she started the car. She knew where she had to go.

Parking on Tremont Street, the site of the first fire, Lana looked up at the structure. It was nothing but a burned out husk of a building, looking gray and eerie in the setting sun.

Lana grabbed up another plastic bag from her glove compartment, a stash that Kate had given her. She exited her car and walked toward the burned out building. There were strips of yellow tape everywhere, warning of danger. But Lana knew what she was doing.

She made her way inside, looking up at what had once housed many, many people. She'd read in the paper that a ritzy condo builder had bought the land. He was going to put in expensive condos.

A rustling sound caught her attention and she spun in the fading light. She moved closer, catching a glimpse of something dark. When she got to the area where she thought she'd seen the outline of a man, she stopped. There was no one in sight.

Spooked, she quickly made her way to the place where she thought the basement would be. She shined her flashlight around the area and gasped. Kneeling down, she ran her hand over what had once been the concrete floor of the building's basement. Spalling. Her gut clenched. How could Bryant have missed this twice? She set down the flashlight, pulling the plastic evidence bag out of her pocket. She reached toward the earth and scooped up some dirt. Bringing the bag back toward her, she went to seal it.

Someone shoved her from behind. She sprawled forward, her hands getting scraped against the ground as she braced her fall.

A voice lashed out at her.

"Mind your own business, bitch!"

5

LANA LAY STILL FOR A MOMENT, trying to regain her equilibrium. She started when a voice boomed out of the darkness.

"What the hell are you doing, Dempsey?"

That was Bryant's voice. A light glowed over her and she turned her head. Her eyes protested the brightness and she shielded her eyes.

"Could you get that light out of my eyes, Bryant?"

Forgetting about her hand, she rose, pushing herself off the ground. "You pushed me."

He reared back, his face looking twisted in the eerie dimness.

"You're crazy. I didn't push you."

"You're a liar." Too late, she remembered that he outranked her and she added a defiant "Sir."

"What are you doing here?"

"Looking for clues to prove my point."

His mouth twisted into an ugly grin. "I have had enough of you undermining me and my authority. I'm talking to your captain."

"Go ahead. But I would suggest that you never lay your hands on me again."

He got right in her face, but Lana never gave an inch.

"I didn't push you."

"Right," she said, her voice dripping with disbelief.

"I would suggest you go home, Dempsey," he said as he stalked away.

Undaunted, Lana bent down and retrieved her flashlight and the plastic bag. She wasn't leaving here without a sample.

When she got to her car, she stopped in her tracks. The tires facing the curb were slashed. When she walked around to the driver's side, she saw they were slashed, too.

She unlocked the door and settled into the driver's seat. Her hands tingled from the scrapes. Turning on the overhead light in the car, she inspected the abrasions. Not too bad and they'd only bled a little. She snapped off the light.

Cursing Bryant for his pettiness, she picked up her cell phone and was just about to dial information to call AAA when it rang.

"Hello."

"Hi, Lana."

"Sean, I need you."

There was a pause at the other end of the line. She heard his intake of breath and she could imagine the heat of him, remember the way he'd touched her last night. Filled her to overflowing.

His voice lowered and he said with a teasing note, "Tell me when and where, sweetheart, and I'll be there."

The sound of his voice sent a thrill along her nerve endings.

With amusement and a little teasing of her own, she said, "Actually, all I need right now is a ride."

"What kind of ride?"

She laughed because she couldn't help herself. "You are very bad."

"Let me show you how bad I can really be."

"Unless you come and pick me up, I won't be able to let you show me anything."

"Car trouble?"

"Yes."

"Where are you?" She was amazed at how his voice changed to all business.

"Tremont Street."

"What's the num…Tremont? The site of last week's fire?"

"Yes."

He sighed. "Lana, don't tell me you're investigating."

"Just a little bit."

"We'll discuss what that means when I get there."

Lana was still sitting in her car when Sean arrived about fifteen minutes later. He parked behind her and got out. Walking over to the driver's side of her car, he bent over. In an instant, he jerked open the car door. He crouched. Her face was soot covered, her clothes filthy and there was blood on her blouse. "Damn, what happened?"

"I was gathering evidence and someone pushed me down."

"Who?" His tone hardened and anger ran like wildfire through him.

"I think it was Bryant. But he said he didn't push me and to give him his due, I didn't really see him. It could have been someone else."

"There's blood on your shirt."

Lana swung her hand around. "When I got pushed, I scraped my hands breaking my fall."

Sean took her hands and peered at them.

She pulled them away. "They're not that bad."

"Let's get you home. I've called for a tow."

She cupped his face. "Thanks. That was very thoughtful."

"Lana, promise me that if you're going to collect samples after dark, you'll let me tag along."

"I don't need a bodyguard."

"It's smart and safer to let me tag along."

"You're not asking me to stop?"

"Lana, we've been friends for a long time. Asking you to stop when you have your teeth into something would be fruitless.''

"Sean, this sample will tell me if there's accelerants in the soil. It will connect these two fires. The arsonist is deliberately setting fires from the basement and the middle of the building.''

"He's trying to trap the residents inside.''

"Exactly.''

"What about Bryant? Have you told him your suspicions?''

"Bryant wouldn't listen to me. He insists that the spalling is just from the structure collapse. He doesn't believe there is any connection.''

"Let's talk about this some more. The tow truck is here.'' Sean helped Lana out of the car and she smiled up at him.

"I can walk.''

"I know that, but it feels good to touch you.'' He watched the smile on her face grow wider.

"You know just what to say, O'Neill.''

He bent down and kissed her on the lips. "I try.''

She went to talk to the tow truck driver.

It didn't take long for Sean to drive her home. When he pulled up in front of her house, he wasn't sure whether he should accompany her. If they were still friends:..they *were* friends, but if they were still *only* friends he would have just gone in. Now he felt as if he shouldn't make a move unless she invited him.

Lana got out, and then peered back in when he didn't open his door.

"Aren't you coming in? I mean...if you want to."

"I do. I just...wasn't sure."

"Sean, come on."

She opened the front door and they stepped into her foyer.

Sean said, "How about I give you a bath."

"Don't you want to join me?"

"No, I want to pamper you. You're the one who has been through something."

"I thought you had lawn work to do today for your father."

"I never got to it."

"Why?"

"Other things, plus my mother needed a present for my grandmother's birthday."

"So you spent time shopping for your grammy?"

He slapped her on the bottom and she laughed. "I didn't mind."

Jumping forward, she called back. "If you beat me to the bathroom, I won't rib you anymore about your grammy."

He surged ahead, bumping into her. But Lana wasn't one to lose graciously. She pushed and bumped him until they were both laughing like fools. Lana saw her opening and darted into the bathroom just before he did.

"I should have taken you more seriously, especially when I've seen what you're like when we get to a fire and you want the hose."

"That's right O'Neill. I'm a force to be reckoned with."

He smiled, grabbed her around the waist and lifted her off the floor to bring her level for direct eye contact. "I like your kind of force and I'll give you all the reckoning you want. Any way you want it."

"I can think of so many ways," she said softly as she wrapped her legs around his waist.

"You like sex games, Lana?"

"With you, Sean, I think I would like just about anything you could dream up."

"I've got a fertile imagination."

"Among other very nice attributes."

He smiled. "Are you flirting with me, Dempsey?"

"As you know, I can be very straightforward with what I want. I'm no shrinking violet."

"Nope, you make that abundantly clear every day."

Her eyes narrowed. "Are you saying that's a bad thing?"

"No. I'm just saying that you don't have to prove anything to me, sweetheart."

She sighed. "No, I've never had to, that's true. You've always accepted that I'm a woman—"

"Amen to that."

That got her to smile, "—in a man's job."

"I don't have any complaints. Wasn't it you who pulled me out of a collapsing, burning building?" He set her down.

"Yes, I guess I did. I was very happy to do so."

Lana had set up dozens of candles all around the bathroom and she lit each one.

The interior of the bathroom took on a warm, golden glow. She bent over to turn on the tap and he stilled her hand. "Let me do that for you." He patted the edge of the tub. "You sit here and relax."

Lana sat down and waited patiently.

Sean turned on the tap, testing the water with his wrist, adjusting the temperature until he had it just right. He turned to her and reached out. He grasped the hem of her T-shirt and pulled it over her head.

She was wearing a red lace bra, very feminine. It cupped her breasts, showing him the shadowy outline of her nipples that peaked as he looked at her. He took her hands and lifted her from the rim of the tub. Gently he unsnapped her jeans and slid them down her legs. Red lace thong panties covered the thatch of hair between her legs, but left her buttocks bare. The sight of her luminous skin hardened his cock until it butted up against the placard of his jeans.

The candles flickered and danced as his breath

whooshed in. "Do you wear this kind of underwear under your uniform?"

"I don't know if I should answer that question."

"Why?"

"I don't want you to be distracted by imagining what I'm wearing underneath my uniform when you should be concentrating on the job."

"Too late."

"What does that mean?"

"I've been thinking that ever since I set eyes on you." He ran his hand around the lace of the panties and his body hardened further when he heard her gasp.

"Really."

"I tried to keep my thoughts on other things, but when not in the heat of battle, I wondered what was under that uniform."

"I don't know. There's nothing more tantalizing than anticipation. I should keep you guessing."

"You're a cruel woman, Lana."

She smiled, reached out and caressed his cheek, her hand going into his hair. His scalp tingled and his body tightened, the wonderful ache spreading through his system.

"I'll put you out of your misery. I wear this kind of underwear all the time. My drawers are full of it. It makes me feel like a woman even though I have to wear the uniform."

"I know I'm supposed to look past gender and

be a new millennium guy, but Lana, I could never think of you in any other way. You don't need underwear to be sexy. You just are."

She closed her eyes and slipped her arms around his waist, pressing her face to his chest.

"Sean, that has to be the most beautiful thing anyone has ever said to me."

That admission stripped him to the quick. He realized there was so much that he didn't know about Lana. But standing here with her, he knew that he wanted to know everything.

Within the soft glow of the candles, they seemed wrapped in a silent, steady flame.

His heart missed a beat, a sudden ache jamming in his throat. What if he messed up? One mistake and he could lose her forever. It was a risk he hadn't been willing to take before.

But she had blown him away in the station shower. Bold and daring, she'd walked right up to him and had stated in straightforward terms that she wanted him.

He couldn't help it. He was still worried about where they would go. What this intense feeling would metamorphosize into.

He knew only one thing. He couldn't lose her.

"It's true. You're all woman all the time. Don't try to be a woman doing a man's job. Just be who you are. There's never any danger in that."

"Sean," she said raising her head. "I had no idea you were a philosopher."

"I do what I can," he said wryly and she chuckled against his chest.

She pressed her cheek hard against his chest as she tightened her arms around his waist, rubbing her body against his. He felt her tremble. He placed a kiss on the top of her head, and then slid his fingers along her scalp, cradling her head in his firm grip. The heavy, silky weight of her hair tangled around his fingers, the loose fall like satin against her shoulders. Sean closed his eyes and hugged her hard, a swell of emotion making his chest tighten.

Only in this moment did he realize the way she filled a hole inside him.

He felt her sigh and he smoothed one hand across her hips and up her back. Easing in a breath of his own, he brushed a kiss against her ear, then spoke, his voice gruff and uneven. "Do you have any idea what you do to me?"

He tucked his head down against hers and drew her hips flush against him. "You feel so good against me."

A tremor coursed through her, and Lana dragged her arms free and slipped them around his neck, the shift intimately and fully aligning her body against his. Sean drew an unsteady breath and angled her head back, making a low, indistinguishable sound as he covered her mouth in a kiss that was raw with desire, governed by the need to make it more than lust, more than need.

Lana went still. Then, with a soft exhalation, she clutched at him and yielded to his deep, hot kiss. Sean slid his hand along her jaw, his callused fingers snagging in the long silky strands of her hair as he altered the angle of her head. She moved against him. Sean shuddered and tightened his hold, a fever of emotion sluicing through him.

Dragging his mouth away, he trailed a string of kisses down her neck, then caught her head again and gave her another hot, wet kiss. His breathing ragged, he tightened his hold on her face and drew back, holding her against his chest. He held her like that, his hand cupping the back of her neck, until his breathing evened out. Then he turned, tucking her against him as he moved slightly away from her.

He reached down and turned off the tap. "Let's get you in the tub." He reached around her and un-snapped her red-hot bra. Her breasts spilled out and it was all he could do not to cup them, rub his thumbs around her exquisite nipples.

He took off her panties, her hand going to his shoulder for balance.

When he stood, she dipped her hand in the frothy water and splashed it down the front of his shirt.

"Oh, look at that. You're shirt's all wet. You couldn't possibly wear it now."

Sean smiled. "Do you want me to take my shirt off?"

She stepped into the tub, sighing as the warm water closed over her body. "Whatever gave you that idea?"

He laughed. "All you had to do was ask."

"You made me wet, so I returned the favor."

He stilled and looked down at her. "It's a good thing you didn't tell me that while you were out here."

"I take it I wouldn't have gotten my bath."

"No, you wouldn't have." He took off his T-shirt and dropped it on the floor and knelt down.

Leaning against the edge of the tub, he put on a loofah bath mitt from the basket on the lip of the tub and squeezed a generous amount of bath gel on it.

He started at her glorious neck and gently massaged the soap into her skin, then moved to her shoulders. The very ones she'd used to carry him. He moved across her collarbones. The heat from the bath had put color in her cheeks. She looked flushed and aroused, her heavy lidded eyes watching him like sparks in a burning ember, hot and smoldering.

Without warning he swept across one of her nipples and Lana moaned, arching her back against the roughness applied to her sensitive skin.

"Tell me if it hurts," he whispered against the perfect shell of her ear.

"Sean," she managed, "It hurts so good. Don't stop."

He slid the mitt over her other breast and Lana grabbed his wrist, caressing his forearm and the bulge of his biceps. Her leg came up and the water rippled with her movement.

His erection swelled inside his jeans. Her response was like nectar on his tongue, so sweet.

He dragged the cloth across her stomach beneath the water then down her leg. She bucked when he swept the cloth across her inner thigh. Her tongue came out to moisten her beautiful lips, so finely shaped. He picked up her ankle and lifted her foot out of the tub. He washed the top of her foot and then the sole. Lana moaned softly. He bent forward and placed his lips against the sole of her foot and kissed his way around to the instep.

He placed her foot back in the water and then picked up her other one. He did the same. Sean took the mitt off and grabbed the detachable showerhead. He turned it on.

"Lana, stand up."

She opened her eyes and rose out of the water. Sean moved close to her and took one pink puckered nipple into his mouth and sucked hard. Lana cried out and arched her back. "Spread your legs," he whispered, after letting her nipple go.

She did, lost in the sensation of his mouth closing over her other nipple. His free hand went to the small of her back as he directed the jet spray against her most sensitive flesh.

Lana writhed in his arms as he suckled her, bit her gently, and tongued her nipples. It wasn't long before she threw her head back and sobbed his name as she came apart in his arms.

Her knees buckled and he set her gently into the water, turning off the shower and then gathering her up in his arms.

She was shaking like a leaf by the time they made it to the bedroom, and he paused by the bed, letting her slick body slide down his. He brought her against him hard. Pressing his face against the curve of her neck, he embraced her, trying to keep at bay the savage need trying to overpower his control.

Taking several deep breaths, he clenched his teeth and tipped his head back. Somehow he got his wet jeans off without letting her go. He managed to tear open the small foil packet and sheath himself.

He was shaking nearly as badly as she when he lifted her onto the bed, then followed her down. He dragged her beneath him. The feel of her plump breasts made him groan. He wanted to be inside her. Deep inside her tight sheath. Feeling as if his heart would burst, as if his lungs would seize up, he probed her with his thick erection. She made a small, frantic noise and opened her legs, urging him forward with single-minded purpose. Sean clenched his jaw and closed his eyes, burying himself deep inside her.

He tightened his arms around her, a jolt of pure pleasure vibrating through him. He ground his teeth together, the sensory assault nearly tearing him apart. It wasn't the act of joining with her that was overpowering, but the intimate connection, as if being inside her merged them into one complete whole. Immobile with the electrifying rush of sensation, he released a shaky sigh, bracing his weight on his forearms. Cupping her face in his hands, his heart ensnared, he covered her mouth in a slow, wet, kiss.

Lana clutched at him, lifting her hips and rotating her pelvis hard against him. Sean roughly slid his arm under her lower back, working his mouth hungrily against hers. He elevated her hips, and then twisted his hips against hers.

Lana gasped brokenly. Sean absorbed her response, a red haze clouding his mind when Lana countered his thrust, her body shuddering beneath him.

Sean tore his mouth away, breathing hard, knowing he had to hold on to give her as much pleasure as he could. He thrust hard into her, not giving her time to catch her breath.

She made a fierce sound and her counterthrusts turned reckless and erratic, and Sean took her nipple in his mouth and sucked hard. The hot taste of her sending his senses into overdrive. He plunged his face into the curve of her neck and thrust into her, keeping the hard edge of his need under control.

Lana jackknifed beneath him, and Sean's face contorted with the torturous pleasure as her inner muscles squeezed around him, milking him. Then with a ragged groan, he went rigid in her arms and let go, emptying himself deep inside her.

Embracing her, he gasped at the feeling of being turned inside out. Pressing his mouth against her temple, he closed his eyes, his pulse choppy and erratic. The feelings in his chest were almost too much to handle.

He drew a deep, shaky breath and pressed an impassioned kiss against her parted lips. The sweep of his tongue, slow and comforting as he softly stroked the angle of her jaw with his thumb. Taking a deep breath, he bracketed her face with his hands, shifting his weight so his hips settled deeper against her.

She spoke in a shaky whisper. "That was so amazing. It's never been like this for me, Sean."

He closed his eyes, emotion clogging in his throat. "Me, neither," he said gruffly.

He rolled onto his back. After a moment, she placed her hand on his chest and he turned his face toward her.

"Before this goes any further, I have to tell you something." Lana released her breath, her expression sober. She stared down at him, the faint light from the living room casting shadows on her face.

He looked into her pensive brown eyes and what he saw there made his heart lurch. Had he gone too far somehow, breached barriers that Lana hadn't wanted him to breach? Was she going to tell him it was over?

"Sean, please remember that I did this in the heat of the moment before I thought...."

Sean experienced a rush of emotion. Suddenly, the light mood was totally gone, replaced by something foreboding. He'd wondered how long it would be before the bubble burst and reality would sweep in, and all this magic would disappear. "What is it, Lana?" he asked.

She stared at him for a second, something akin to fear flashing across her eyes, then regret. "I seduced you on a dare I have with Sienna and Kate."

Feeling as if she'd pulled the ground out from under him, he stared at her. It was as if she'd peeled away some protective layer, leaving him without any defenses, and blood rushed to his ears.

"A dare?" he repeated stupidly. "For what?"

She swallowed. "A souvenir."

"What kind of souvenir?"

"A sexy one."

"I see. So this was only about sex?"

"Yes—I mean no. Let me explain."

"You don't have to." He got off the bed, grabbed

up his clothes and rushed to dress, almost putting out all the candles.

And he thought that she was treating him just like everybody else—good old Sean won't mind. Well, he did mind. He minded a whole hell of a lot. No more, he thought as he threw on his clothes and splashed cold water on his face. He wasn't going to be easygoing Sean anymore.

The scent of the room had been a sexual goad, now it was a painful reminder of his stupid idyllic dreams. It was only now he realized how deep his feelings for Lana went. Down to his heart.

When he returned to Lana, she was still sitting on the bed, draped in nothing but the sheet. Her body was a combination of sleek strength and womanly curves.

"Sean, if you give me a moment to explain. We were at a club and we were drinking. Sienna walked in with this hunk and I dared her to go after him. Before I knew it, I had agreed to go after you."

He drew his eyes from her and without another word, left the room.

The hurt sluiced through him as deep and as devastating as the pleasure had only a few moments before.

6

LANA SCRAMBLED OFF THE BED, the hurt look in his eyes arrowing straight to her heart. She grabbed at her clothes.

"Sean, wait!" she yelled. Pulling a shirt over her head and hopping into her jeans, she rushed for the door.

"Sean!" she cried. But he was already striding across her living room and the sound of the slamming door was his only response.

She closed her eyes and leaned against the jamb, her throat thick with emotions. Damn, damn and double damn. Why couldn't he just stop and listen to her?

His car started, a loud angry noise in the still night. She made it to the window in just enough time to see his taillights disappear into the darkness.

For the first time since she met him, her world tilted out of kilter. The power of Sean's friendship had kept her grounded. Unsettled by that thought, she regretted the cavalier way she'd treated this whole souvenir thing with him.

Okay, so she had initially thought he would

chuckle and hand over a souvenir, but she'd obviously been wrong about his reaction.

Seriously wrong.

Reaching down, she snagged her phone and pressed number one on her speed dial—Sean's cell. The phone rang, but he didn't answer.

She hung up and then pressed two. Sienna's sleepy voice came over the line, "'lo."

"Sienna, it's Lana."

Her friend's voice strengthened and she said, "What's the matter?"

"Let me get Kate on three-way and I'll explain. I only want to do this once," Lana said.

When Kate answered, Lana began to launch into her explanation. But before she could get too far, Kate said, "I'm coming over there."

Sienna said, "I'll meet you there."

Both women hung up before Lana could say a word.

They got to her house shortly after midnight, just fifteen minutes after she'd called them. When they came through the door, they hugged Lana in turn.

Comfortably ensconced on her couch, Sienna asked, "So tell us what happened?"

"Sean and I just had this mind-blowing sex. Afterward, I got to feeling guilty that I started a sexual relationship with Sean on a dare. I knew I had to tell him. I should have told him right up-front…"

"Why did you have to tell him at all and why in bed?" Sienna asked with a scolding tone.

"I agree that right after sex was a poor judgment call, but I wasn't thinking. I just knew that I had to be honest with him. What if the information came out later and I hadn't told him? How do you think he'd feel then?"

"Worse," Kate said.

"Is he mad?" Sienna asked.

"I wish. I think I could deal with it better if he were. No, he's hurt."

"What are you going to do?" Kate asked.

"I don't know. I have to, at the very least, apologize to him." Lana cradled her head in her hands. "I'm worried he won't want to be friends with me anymore. Why did I have to be so stupid? Nothing is ever as simple as it seems."

Kate leaned forward and squeezed Lana's arm. "If Sean really cares for you, he'll forgive you. You might have to grovel, but it would be worth it. Right?"

"Yes. Anything to change that awful look in his eyes," Lana agreed.

"Are you in love with him?" Sienna asked point-blank.

"We've been friends since the academy." Lana realized that she hadn't really thought about it.

"What kind of answer is that?" Sienna said.

"What's wrong with that answer?"

"You didn't answer her question," Kate said gently.

Lana sighed. "Sean and I are friends. It's really all we can be."

"Is that all you want?" Kate said.

"I don't know. I'm on the fast track to captain and Sean is a squad member. There could be complications from that. I can't let anything stand in the way of my dream. It's what I've always wanted."

Sienna sat forward. "Is it so black and white?"

"Sounds clear cut to me," Lana said. "Look, you guys better get out of here. I could talk to you all night, but you both have to work. I'm off tomorrow."

"Yes, you have a dream schedule, but a tough job," Kate said.

"I'd do this job for free," Lana said.

"Kate, before you go, I wanted to give you this." Lana stepped over to her purse and pulled out the evidence bag. "Here's the sample we talked about."

Kate took the bag as she rose from the couch. "I can't do this for you until the end of the day tomorrow."

"That's okay. I appreciate you doing it for me at all."

Kate grabbed Lana's hand before she could withdraw it. "What happened to your hands?" Kate demanded, alarm in her voice.

"When I was gathering this evidence, someone

shoved me down in the dirt. When I got back to my car, my tires were slashed.''

Sienna rose from the couch. Eyeing Lana, she straightened. Her face was flushed and there was a furious glint in her eye. ''Who do you think it was?''

''Bryant was there, but I can't prove he shoved me. The guy caught me from behind.''

''But who do you think it was?'' Sienna persisted.

''I think it was Bryant.''

''Why do you think it was him?'' Sienna asked.

''He whispered, 'Mind your own business, bitch.' ''

''Sure sounds like him,'' Kate said, looking worried. ''You need to be more careful.''

Sienna's eyes narrowed, her voice tough as steel, ''Want me to pay him a visit?''

Lana smiled. ''No, I can handle Bryant and from now on I'll be more careful.''

''You're still going to pursue this?'' Sienna asked.

''I have to because Bryant doesn't believe it's a serial arsonist and I do.''

''Okay, but if you need me, let me know. Be careful.''

''I will.''

Sienna opened the front door and stepped through, but Kate hesitated at the doorway. She put her hand on Lana's arm.

''Friends are friends,'' Kate said with a small

smile. "Sometimes they fight and get mad at each other, but make up. It'll be fine."

"I hope so. The last thing I wanted to do was hurt Sean."

"Did you think about why he reacted this way? He must have pretty strong feelings for you."

Kate squeezed her arm and turned toward the porch. She stepped out and Lana watched as she got into her car.

She had been preoccupied with thinking about Sean's obvious hurt and not why he was hurt. They were good friends and she should have taken that into consideration before she'd gone ahead and seduced him. Although Sean was her friend, their relationship had been volatile from the beginning. She'd always been attracted to him, but now she was just realizing that maybe Sean hadn't explored his feelings for her.

Then she'd blindsided him.

Unsettled by the emotion, confused by her own feelings, Lana headed back to her room. There was one consolation in that Sean was just as confused as she was. Maybe he needed time to work through it by himself. Once he did that, they could go back to normal.

Whatever that was.

LANA TRIED TO GET SEAN on the phone all the next day while she picked up her dry cleaning, cleaned her house, and washed her car, but he wasn't picking up.

The truth of the matter was that before she had seduced Sean in the shower, they'd tiptoed around each other, careful never to acknowledge the sexual tension that crackled whenever they were close. Did they each sense that it would complicate their lives, their working relationship, and their friendship. That didn't take much brain power. Of course, they did.

Lana finally gave up at about six o'clock and decided a game of pool, conversation and a cold beer would sit well with her. She knew she could always get some action from the guys at Mahoney's. Firefighters had made that bar their home away from home along with the boys and girls in blue.

The bar was dim, crowded and very noisy. Lana stood in the doorway giving her eyes time to adjust and looking for people she knew. Spying some people in the corner, she wound her way through the maze of tables.

Lana slapped a man on the back when she reached the table. He turned his head and gave her a full grin.

"Hey, Dempsey, good to see you."

Scott Mason had been onē of her father's probie's when he'd been at the eighty-second. He was now in his forties and a veteran firefighter.

His wife Susan smiled at Lana and moved over

to make room for Lana to sit down at the crowded table.

Also at the table was SDPD patrol cop Rosa Santana, a six-foot formidable Hispanic Amazon. Her burly boyfriend firefighter, Steven Anderson, a wet behind the ears probie at the eighty-second sat next to her. Although he was young and eager, he was also very good.

And Pete Meadows sat at the end of the table, rounding out the party at six people. He smiled at Lana and raised his bottle.

Steven eyed Lana and smiled. "Heard you pulled O'Neill and two victims out of Monday's four-alarm. Went through a wall to get them out. Would have liked to been on duty when that alarm came through."

"It was hairy there for a while, but we got everyone out."

"Always good when you save all the victims," Steven said.

Pete piped in. "Yeah the sparks were flying around the fire ground, but it was nothing compared to the fireworks between Dempsey and Bryant."

Scott turned to Lana, "Don't tell me you were trying to tell the know-it-all SOB anything. Waste of breath, Lana."

Pete chuckled, and Rosa leaned her arms on the table. "Don't let them give you a hard time. They're just afraid of Bryant's legendary temper." She pointed at Pete, "Get her a beer since you brought it up. Sounds like she deserves it."

Susan Mason raised her empty bottle and moved it from side to side. "You owe me one, too. You passed out before your round last time."

Her husband leaned forward and slapped a twenty-dollar bill on the table. He looked at Lana, a sparkle of amusement in his eyes. "Her beer is on me. I would have given my eyeteeth to see Dempsey standing up to Bryant."

Smiling into his eyes, she tilted her head. "I call them like I see them and Bryant was wrong."

"*Oooooh,*" the three firefighters said in unison.

Steven said, "Telling Bryant he was wrong. I wished I'd been on duty." Steven threw in a twenty. "Her next one is on me."

Susan laughed and applauded. "That is rich. Taking potshots at Bryant's ego. That must have hurt," she said, her eyes bright with delight. "That guy has an ego to rival Napoleon." She looked at Lana, raising her empty bottle in salute. "Congratulations, Lana. About time someone put him in his place."

Lana cocked her head, her expression wry. "It was definitely my pleasure."

The waitress came over and soon after that Lana had a beer in front of her.

"We were just going to play some pool. Check out these new tables Tim put in. You up for it?" Steven asked.

He downed the rest of his beer, and then gave Lana a light jab in the shoulder. "Come on. It'll be quieter in there."

When they got to the back, Steven was right. It was much quieter in there. Five of the six gleaming pool tables were already in use. Lana's group claimed the sixth one. She studied the tables as she passed. Standard billiards tables, but they were high quality. Looks like Tim didn't spare any expense.

The memory of the endless games of pool she'd shared with Sean made her throat tight. Although he wouldn't admit it, she knew he went easy on her. If Sean wasn't such a nice guy, he could have made scads of money as a pool shark.

Rosa didn't want to play, so Lana sat at the table with her, watching the men. After two games, Pete came over to her and leaned toward her. "Don't you want to play, Lana?"

She looked up into Pete's face and smiled at the mischievous grin there. Then her smile faded when she saw Sean standing in the doorway to the pool tables. His gaze riveted to the intimate proximity of Pete's body.

God, he was attractive. Strong, male and capable. So sexy in his tight black shirt and painted-on denim jeans, black cowboy boots on his feet.

His hair was brushed off his face in short, haphazard waves.

Scott called out to Sean. Sean's attention diverted

from her and Pete as he waved and greeted Scott. But his gaze barely shifted from her, as he walked toward them. Sean stood in front of Pete and said, "Could I have a word with you, Lana."

"O'Neill," Pete said, "She's talking to me right now."

"I wasn't talking to you, Meadows." The tone of Sean's voice had the keen edge to it. The chatter between the two men at the pool table ceased as they watched the standoff.

Pete backed up. "Okay, O'Neill. You don't have to get so uptight."

Irritation and heat at Sean's obvious jealousy jetted through her.

Pete retreated and went to the pool tables and conversation started up again.

Sean leaned down until he was very close to her ear. "Looking to get yourself another souvenir?"

Lana stiffened and anger simmered in her gut. Sean withdrew and nodded to Rosa. Picking up Lana's bottle of beer, he took a swig.

She watched as he swallowed, his lips moist from the brew. And she wanted to kiss him, wondering what he would do if she did just that in this crowded bar, in front of their friends. People who had no idea what had transpired between them in the last twenty-four hours.

"I've been trying to reach you."

"I got your messages. I was busy."

"Sean, can I have a few words with you outside?"

"What for, Lana? We were both jerks. Let's leave it at that."

"Sean," Lana said, rising from her chair and laying her hand on his forearm. Her fingers reacted on their own, curling around his hot, male flesh.

"You want to talk to me. I'll play you for it." He said, indicating a newly vacated table.

"Play me...pool?"

"Sure, why not? I think you like games, Lana."

A nasty little flutter took off in Lana's throat, and she felt the blood rush to her middle. It got unnaturally quiet in their corner, and she tried to swallow. She reached out and grabbed a cue. "Fine," she said, her tone flat.

Sean walked over to the table and picked up a cue from the edge and chalked it; then he looked at her, not a trace of expression in his eyes. "Best two out of three."

Still gripping the cue, she nodded. She had to talk to him tonight or his anger would fester and their friendship would be damaged. This was her one chance.

He stared at her for a good ten seconds, then spoke, his tone like steel. "Your break," he said.

She went to the head of the table and with a quick line up and a hard move of her shoulder, the balls scattered, two solids going into pockets. She lined up another shot and sank that ball, too.

"I need to get by," she said. This particular table was a few feet away from the wall and Sean was blocking the space.

"Go ahead," he replied without moving a muscle. It irked her that she either had to walk all the way around the other side of the table or squeeze by him.

"Fine," she countered. Deliberately, she slid her body along his in a slow caress. Sean's smoky-gray eyes flared and narrowed. The heat of his body seeped into her and she hesitated only a fraction of a second before moving on. Unnerved, she missed her shot.

Sean took over the table and he was good. Very good. But she was lucky that his anger was so thick, he missed a ball and Lana took over.

The first game was close. But it was his win.

He never even gave her an opening in the second game.

Without looking at her, he chalked the end of his cue. His face expressionless, he eyed the table. Bending down, his voice curt, he said. "Six ball in the corner pocket."

He proceeded to clear the table of balls, making one impossible shot after another. When he'd taken care of all the solids, he spoke, his voice slicing through the silence. "Eight ball in the side pocket."

With a sharp report of white against black, the black ball flew into the pocket as if spring-loaded.

7

"THAT'S THE WAY TO PUT HER in her place, O'Neill. How about taking on a real man?" Dane Bryant stood close to the table and Lana cursed her luck. She saw the anger in Sean's eyes intensify and focus on Bryant.

That's all she needed was for these two to brawl. Sean took a step, but she deliberately blocked him, feeling the heat of his big, male body come up against her back, his groin nestle against her buttocks.

"A real man doesn't push a woman down and then slash her tires."

"What the hell are you talking about, O'Neill?"

Sean did a dodge around Lana. Before she could stop him, he grabbed Bryant. With the force of a Mac truck, he propelled the man across the room and up against the wall.

"You know what I'm talking about, so don't pretend," Sean said through gritted teeth.

Lana rushed up to them, Rosa flanking her. Lana grabbed Sean's arm and tried to pull him off Bryant. It was like trying to move a concrete foundation.

Even with all Lana's strength, she couldn't budge him.

In a detached part of her brain, she was awed and totally turned on by Sean's strength and protectiveness. She hadn't realized the gentle friend she knew could be so tough.

Lana knew part of it was that he was so angry with her he wanted a fight. She could see it in the taut lines of his body.

"Don't do it, *amigo*," Rosa said softly. "He's not worth a night in jail."

"She's right," Lana said, softly. "Let him go."

Sean held on a moment longer and then let go. Lana grabbed his wrist and jerked him out of the poolroom, through the bar and out into the night.

She pulled him over to her SUV and ordered, "Get in."

Sean stiffened and turned away. "I brought my own car."

She grabbed at his arm. "I can't trust you to go home. I'm afraid you'll go back and kick Bryant's ass."

"Why would you care? You don't even like him!"

"And since when have you been the kind of guy who wants to punch people's lights out instead of being reasonable?" Lana yelled.

"Since things between us became complicated," Sean yelled back.

He got into her car and slammed the door. They

sat for a moment in silence. "I've decided not to be easygoing Sean anymore. I'm the Sean who takes what he wants, when he wants it."

Without warning, Sean reached for her and dragged her across the plastic console, settling her into the cradle of his thighs.

The darkness outside the SUV and the tinted windows kept out most of the light and shielded them from unwanted scrutiny.

"Sean," she whispered against his demanding mouth, but he wouldn't stop kissing her. She tried to pull away to get a word in, but decided that a little sex would soothe the savage beast in him. She was aroused from Sean's display at the pool table and his protective episode with Bryant. Her laid-back buddy was turning into this dark, sexy knight and she liked it. She knew that they couldn't go back to being just friends. The thought of their relationship changing from one that was simple, to this…this out of control intimacy was a bit terrifying. But she would embrace it. It's what she'd really wanted from Sean.

He cupped the nape of her neck and dragged her face to his for another rough, plundering kiss. He pressed her down against his erection, his hands fisting in her hair. Taking her mouth with a deep groan, his hands were hard, insistent, right on the edge of painful, but it was a delicious tingling pain.

She wished she could see his face. Using her hands instead, she reveled in the texture of his skin.

She felt intensely vulnerable, and so excited she could melt into a shimmering cloud. She squirmed against the rock-hard bulge beneath her bottom and kissed him back hungrily.

He vibrated against her, sliding his hand down between the waistband of her jeans and panties and her quivering skin, absorbing the cry with his mouth as he touched her where she so desperately needed to be touched. Lana clutched at him, her body going rigid, and he brought her face against his neck as she involuntarily arched against the stroking pressure of his fingers. An explosion detonated inside her, and a chain of convulsions ripped through her as she came apart.

Sean took a deep breath as Lana climaxed. His feelings were overpowering him right now and he struggled to control the surging, chaotic whirl of his mind and body. He was angry at her, jealous of Pete, furious with Bryant. He wanted to hit something. He wanted to feel the softness of her skin. He wanted to hold her. He wanted to hear her cry his name as she came and came.

He hadn't meant to kiss her, not when the heart-pumping adrenaline coursed through his veins, not with his hunger riding him relentlessly. He'd meant to yell at her and get all this hurt out of his system before he touched her again, but when she came near him now, he couldn't think.

He took her mouth again, dragging her back into the maelstrom of his hunger, not easing up his aggressive attack. And she kissed him back as he drew her fast into their passion again, yet not fast enough for his spiraling need.

Angling his mouth across hers, he pulled at her lower lip. She opened her mouth on a gasp and a groan, deepening the kiss, tongue to tongue, caressing the softness of her sweet mouth.

Her reaction spoke for her as she twisted impatiently against him, one knee sliding over his thigh. Cupping her buttocks, he pulled her hips into his rhythm.

This is what he needed. Lana's fingers in his hair, boldly rubbing his cock through his jeans, jerking at his waistband and working the metal button free. She brushed her knuckles against him, taking him into mindless, dangerous sensation.

It was as if he didn't know himself anymore, as if Lana was defining him, bringing out his true nature. He hadn't known he could feel so much in such a short time.

In her fire, he was a phoenix reborn.

In the fire of their need their relationship was being forged, changed, remade. He couldn't say that he didn't like it. But it terrified him, this uncontrollable feeling he had for Lana.

It wasn't only the relationship that was changing. When Lana told him about the souvenir, he'd known she thought he'd go along. It was the last straw to a life of acquiescence. Even their previous relationship had been tame because he'd never reached for anything more. He'd always held himself back. Not anymore.

Bracing her knees on either side of him she reached down to unzip his jeans, but he grabbed her wrists. "No."

He watched as she stopped abruptly, leaning back. "What…"

"Drive. Now. The sooner you do, the sooner you can slide down on to my cock."

She swallowed and quickly got off his lap. Settling into the driver's seat, she started the car and put it in gear.

Sean had already buttoned his jeans. "I'll follow you."

He got out and went to his car, his body throbbing with a desire so thick he could barely breathe around it. He followed Lana's taillights all the way to her house.

IT DIDN'T TAKE them long to get up the walk, and Lana felt surprised when Sean took her arm and directed her into the garden past the huge sunflowers and fragrant beds until they were out of sight.

She watched as he jerked off his clothes with hard, effective movements. Lana followed his lead, stepping quickly out of her shoes, unbuttoning the clasp of her jeans.

He unbuckled his belt and kicked off jeans, shoes, socks and underwear. He was ready, naked and waiting while she was starting to unbutton her blouse.

Her brown eyes caressed the length of his naked body. He was so beautiful in the moonlight, like a sculpted statue come to life.

She knew the moment when his patience snapped. As he advanced, she smiled coyly and backed away. He kept coming at her until her back hit the side of the bungalow. His hands went to the buttons. In his haste to disrobe her, fabric ripped and buttons popped.

She gasped and moaned softly as he shoved the torn garment off her shoulders. This close she could smell his warm, knee-melting scent.

Her hands caught in the still-buttoned cuffs and he brought them forward and up over her head as he pressed his body against hers.

He nuzzled her breasts, his tongue dipping into her cleavage.

Holding her wrists immobile in one of his big hands, he roughly pulled down one cup of her bra to expose her succulent nipple. With a growl deep in his throat, he took it into his mouth, working it hungrily against his tongue and sucking it. Sensations pounded through her, arrowing into her groin.

"Sean, let go," she whispered. He did, pulling down her other cup and taking her tantalizing nipple into his mouth.

She freed herself of the ruined blouse. Her slender hands ran down his back, over his buttocks, bringing his shaft against the rough material of her jeans.

He cried out. Cursing, he fumbled with the zipper

of her jeans. As soon as the fabric yielded, he slid to his knees, wrenching her jeans down around her ankles. He did the same for the scrap of blue lace covering her sex.

Sean stopped panting. He was shaking, muscles rigid, heart racing. She was overwhelmed with how much he wanted her until it was a hard, spiraling ache inside her. His face was mere inches from the soft curves of her thighs, the tangle of dark curls that hid her sex.

Lana stared down at him. His eyes flared and smoldered, enigmatic in the shadows. Her mouth parted and she licked her dry lips. His eyes were so full of emotion, Lana had to look away.

His tousled hair lifted in the breeze, dislodging a lock that had fallen over his forehead. She steadied herself on his shoulders and her fingers flinched at the contact.

"Sean, you're burning hot."

Her hand slowly caressed his throat, then his face. She explored the bones of his jaw and his cheekbones with the tips of her cool fingers.

He sighed at her touch, closing his eyes and pressing his face against her soft belly. She battled for air, feeling as if her heart were seizing in her chest.

She felt wild and frantic teetering on the very edge of sanity. His cheek was rough against the skin of her belly.

Grasping her ankle, he ran his hand up until he slid between her thighs. Forcing them apart, he pressed his face against her mound. She shuddered and cried out.

Her hands threaded through his hair, clutching tightly as he pressed his mouth against the tender moist folds inside the nest of curls. He tasted her, absorbing the cry that shivered through her body.

He came to his feet, his chest heaving. Clasping her shoulders, he turned her around, gently biting her shoulder blade, deftly unclasping her bra. He slipped the scrap of lace off her shoulders and down her arms. His hands slid back up her rib cage to cup her breasts in his hands.

She twisted in his arms and he leaned down to take one of her beckoning nipples. His hand grabbed her wrist and guided her hand to his cock.

"Touch me, Lana."

"How? Show me."

He directed her hand up and down his shaft in long, hard pulls. He slid her palm around the head, moistening it with a pearly drop of pre-come so that her hand could slide up and down the length of him, slick and silky.

He moved to the other nipple. "Use both hands," he said roughly before taking her other nipple. He groaned when she gripped him with rough eagerness.

"I like it hard," he urged.

"I like it hard, too," she whispered against his ear. Lana made a purring sound, increasing her tempo and dragging a groan of pleasure out of him.

His hands roamed over her eagerly, skimming her soft swells and dips and curves.

With hard, bold strokes, she was drawing him dangerously close to the brink, and how she reveled in her power over him. He had never demanded like this from her and she wanted him to overpower her.

He shoved her back, lifting her up against the rough wall.

She held on to his shoulders for balance. She moaned, almost inaudibly, as he kissed her neck, trailing the tip of his tongue over her damp skin.

Her gaze locked with his as he slid a finger inside her sheath, testing her. He withdrew his finger slowly and circled it around her rosy, swollen nub. "You like that?"

Her fingers dug into his shoulders, her hips jerking against his hand. "Yes," she gasped out.

"You liked touching my cock?" he persisted.

Her hips pulsed eagerly as he slid his gleaming finger in and out of her.

He took a moment to grab up his jeans and get a condom, which he swiftly rolled onto himself, lifting her legs and opening her thighs.

She braced her hands, holding herself upright, watching him, her soft thighs open for him to take what he wanted.

He pushed into her with one slick seamless thrust.

His whole body clenched and he lifted her up against him still thrusting.

Lana cried out. He twisted and they sank into the

bed of flowers deep in the English garden he so loved.

He buried his fingers in her satiny hair and kissed her, a greedy kiss.

She twined her arms around his neck, her hips urging him to move, her body arching and begging beneath him.

Lana moaned softly, her hips bucking as he slid down the length of her body. He pressed her legs toward her chest, opening her. She muffled the shocked cry of pleasure as he drew the swollen center of her pleasure into his mouth.

He took her ruthlessly. Sucking and licking at her, he was deliberately intensifying her need as she twisted in his grasp.

She climaxed gainst his mouth. The spasms beat wet, hot and uncontrollable through her body.

Sean mounted her, settling his hips into her soft, moist sheath.

Lana arched and her eyes flew open as he filled her, pushing into her until he couldn't go any farther.

Her hips rose up to meet him as he pulled out of her and slid, slowly back in.

She slipped her hands into his hair, pulling his head toward her so that she could give him her mouth.

She was his in every sense.

He made her surrender and take the closeness they shared even higher than Lana thought was possible.

The hard, pulsing heat of his cock swept away the last vestiges of her self-control.

"More. Harder, please, Sean."

He plunged in again, her cries sharp and breathless.

She loved the way he thrust mindlessly, caught up in his own body's primal need. Her world splintered into hard-edged pleasure as she lost her footing, and her pleasure detonated through her with brutal force.

He lay on top of her for a moment and then he rolled to the side. After a few moments, they silently dressed and went into her house.

LATER, Lana brushed a few errant strands of hair from her face. "Why were you so angry?" her voice hushed out.

He closed his eyes and responded, "I thought I understood our relationship."

"You're angry because you felt more for me and you thought I didn't care as much?"

"Yes. I feel like I'm on shaky ground."

"It scares you?"

"It does scare me. But what I really don't know how to handle is the fact that I'm some prize in a dare with your girlfriends. I thought I was much more than that to you."

"You are."

"Then why treat me like that?"

She raised herself up on one elbow to look down

into his face. "Did it ever occur to you that it was unnerving to want to make love with a man I consider my best friend? I took that dare, pushed Sienna and Kate because I wanted you."

Sean took a deep breath and looked away.

"Jeez, Lana you know how to take the wind out of a man's sails. What am I supposed to say to that?"

"You don't have to say anything. I was trying to explain to you my convoluted logic. I'm trying to apologize."

"I can understand how you feel. I've thought about you in bed so many times I've lost count. Even when it was contained in my head, it was still unnerving. How would it work between us, if our romantic relationship ended? Hell, we work together."

"I know but when you want someone, there's no logic to it. It just is. I tricked myself into thinking that this dare would work and I could have you once and that would be it. But after the last time with you, I knew that I had to tell you why I really seduced you."

"Because of the need for a souvenir?"

"No. Because I couldn't admit to myself that I wanted you, but it goes beyond sex now."

"When did it change?"

"When I saw that hurt look on your face. I couldn't bear it because I care about you on so many levels."

"So I think we're on the same wavelength. We both care. Where do we go from here?"

"I don't know."

"That's okay, Lana. We don't need to map every nuance and plan for everything. Just don't leave me out of the loop."

"I won't do it again."

"So, we're okay?" he asked wanting to end the animosity between them.

"Yes." She touched his face, looking at him in awe.

"What?" he said.

"I haven't been that turned on or that satisfied ever. It seemed to me that we were both on a path to something special."

"You aren't kidding. I can't say you bring out the worst in me, because, sweetheart there wasn't anything bad about what we just shared."

"Sean, the bad boy lover. Hard for me to get my brain around that one. You're mild-mannered by day, but a man of steel at night."

He laughed and drew her over his body. "I'll show you how hard I can get."

"Now you're talking," she purred.

THE NEXT MORNING AS SEAN LEFT, he passed her father coming up the walk. They nodded to each other warily and Lana closed her eyes.

She'd totally forgotten that her father was going to help her tune up her car today.

When he came into the house, he gave her his we-need-to-talk look and Lana said, ''Don't start.''

''Who was that?''

She held up her hand to stop him. ''Dad. I said don't start.''

''He looked familiar,'' her father said, his eyes narrowing in concentration.

Lana sighed. He would remember. Her father's memory was excellent. ''I work with him.''

He gave a surprised grunt and looked out the window as Sean got into his car. ''At the eighty-second? Are you crazy?''

''I think so,'' Lana said under her breath.

Her father was sober as he regarded her, a worried look in his eyes. ''You shouldn't get involved with anyone on the squad. How can you effectively lead if you've slept with…''

''Dad, drop it. Don't you think I'm smart enough to know that what you're saying is correct. Just let me deal with it in my own way.'' She hadn't admitted it to herself until her father had spelled it out for her. Now she couldn't deny the truth. She would eventually have to break it off with Sean.

He rubbed at his forehead in a frustrated move Lana knew so well. ''You're not thinking, Lana. It has everything…''

Lana glared at him. ''Look, I'm not up to doing the car today. Can we do it some other time?''

''Is that a subtle way of asking me to leave?''

''I don't want to argue with you, Dad. Don't

worry about my commitment to becoming captain. That hasn't changed. I won't let anything stand in the way of realizing my dream, I'll handle it when the time comes.''

After her father left the house, Lana sat down on the rumpled bed and put her head in her hands. What a complicated mess. Why couldn't she have Sean and be captain, too? With a sense of uneasiness, she knew that somewhere down the road she might have to choose. Why did she have to sacrifice him to her ambitions?

She was too drawn to Sean, too aware, too interested in him for her own good. The best thing she could do—the smartest thing—was retreat. But how could she? Their relationship would never be brought to what it once was.

Sean was more than her friend now.

But what that meant, she still wasn't sure.

8

THE MINUTE THAT LANA WALKED into the station she heard her captain call her name.

She poked her head into his office, "Cap?"

For the first time since she'd worked for him, he looked at her sternly. "Sit down."

She took the chair even though she would much rather stand. It was hard to ignore the pictures that covered the walls. Her great-grandfather, grandfather, and father were all members of this station. Her father was the only one who hadn't made captain. She felt the weight of that tradition more so than ever. Perhaps it was the looming test that would take her up to the next level or the secret investigation that was no secret. There was a real possibility she could get a written reprimand.

"Are you stepping all over Dane Bryant's toes?" Captain Troy demanded.

"Yes," she said firmly, "But..."

"I don't want to hear any buts," he snapped. "It's not like you to step out of bounds, Dempsey."

"I collected soil samples and one of the samples

has come back positive for accelerant. I think the second one will, too.''

His face settled in grim lines. ''You do?''

''Yes, sir.''

Her captain grimaced. ''So what were you trying to prove? That Dane was wrong.''

''No, sir,'' she said calmly. ''I was trying to prove that those two fires were deliberate arson and that we have a serial arsonist on our hands.''

He sat back and steepled his fingers. ''Sounds like you are trying to prove Bryant wrong. You can't go around freelancing. Take what you've discovered over to him and leave the investigation to the people who get paid to do it.''

Lana schooled her face into a mask of indifference. ''Yes, sir.''

''Because of your family's long tradition with the fire department, I'm going to cut you some slack. Next time, this goes into your jacket.''

She gave him a quick, jerky nod. ''Yes, sir.''

''Dempsey, has he threatened you?''

''Bryant?'' she asked.

''Yes.''

''No.''

His face hardened. ''I've heard differently.''

''It's not anything I can't handle, sir.''

''There's nothing I'd like to do more than squeeze Bryant's balls in a vise.''

She couldn't completely stop the smile itching to

spread across her face, but it wouldn't be prudent to smile. "Yes, sir, but I can handle it."

"Get going," he said gruffly. "I don't want to be short staffed. Take a man with you, so that you can avoid any unpleasantness."

Lana walked out of the captain's office and almost ran into Sean.

"What happened?" he asked eyeing the captain through the glass.

Lana sighed. "Bryant told on me. I got chewed out and I'm directed to turn the evidence over to Bryant."

"With the evidence that Kate uncovered, you can at least prove that there is a possibility of a serial arsonist."

He said the words to comfort her, but she wasn't happy. "I can, but will Bryant care?"

"Lana, it's not your job to worry about that," he offered.

"I know, but I have a bad feeling about all this." And she did. She didn't think it would do an ounce of good to give this evidence to Bryant. She was convinced that he didn't give a fig what she said. He saw her as a woman who didn't belong in a man's job and who couldn't do that job. Lana sighed. Sean was right. There wasn't anything she could do.

"Let's go get the report from Kate and get over to HQ."

They took one of the station's small trucks to the Police Department to pick up the report.

Kate was in her office when Lana and Sean walked in. Kate smiled at them and indicated her chairs.

"San Diego has a serial arsonist on its hands."

Jolted by her words, Lana felt something come alive inside her, like a wire suddenly filled with electricity. She chafed at the thought that she had to give her hard-won evidence over to a man who could care less. The urge to take the next step in the investigation was almost overpowering. But a bad mark on her record would effectively delay her ascent or may even hurt her enough that the captain's position would move beyond her reach. She shifted, thinking about her father's reaction to that. "Positive for accelerants?"

Kate nodded grimly. "I'm afraid so and they match in quality. I'd say that the two buildings were torched using a metal can like one would use to fill a gas tank. I found trace amounts of metal and rust."

"Any way to trace where the accelerant originated?" Sean asked.

"No. I'm afraid not," Kate said regretfully. "But if you bring me the metal container, I can tell you if it's the one that held the accelerants used in the arsons."

"Thanks, Kate," Lana offered.

Kate pulled her report off the printer and tucked

it into an envelope. She handed it to Lana. After a moment, she said, "Lana, I would suggest that you turn this over to Bryant. It's important information that he should have even though he didn't want to believe you in the first place."

"That's exactly where I'm heading now. I got the word from my captain. No more investigating or else it goes in my file."

"I'm sorry, Lana, but I have to agree with him. This could be very dangerous."

The receptionist in Bryant's office building directed Lana and Sean to the arson investigator's office.

Lana went up to his door and knocked. A man was walking by.

"If you're looking for Dane, he's not here."

"I need to drop off two reports."

"I can take them if you like. What's your name?"

"Dempsey."

"The firefighter who's busting his chops?"

"Afraid so."

Lana felt Sean stiffen beside her and she rested her hand on his arm.

The man laughed and reached out his hand. "Hi, I'm Tim Davis. Keep up the good work."

"Nobody likes the guy," Sean said under his breath.

Lana elbowed him gently in the ribs.

Tim walked to Bryant's office and opened the

door. "Go ahead and leave the stuff on his desk. He'll see it when he gets back."

Lana set the reports on the desk, but photos sitting on top in an open file folder caught her eye.

"Are these from the fires?" Lana asked.

"They are," Tim replied.

"I sure would like to look through them."

She reached for the photos, but Tim stopped her.

"I've got a duplicate set I can lend you as long as you return them."

"You don't mind."

He smiled. "No. I'm the photographer. I think it's good that firefighters take a look. Sometimes you guys see something the arson investigator can't. After all, you're right there in the action."

Lana followed the guy to his office and he handed her a folder.

"It sure seems strange that Bryant's so reluctant to accept evidence that you've collected and had analyzed. Seems it would make his job easier," Tim said.

"That's what I thought," Lana concurred.

BACK IN THE TRUCK, Lana turned to Sean. "Do you think that Bryant could be the arsonist?"

"What?"

"Listen for a moment. He's been hostile about me collecting evidence, won't accept that the fires are connected, and complained to my captain."

Sean shook his head and snorted. "I think he's an uptight jerk who doesn't like women firefighters. Jeez, his own co-workers don't even like him."

Lana heard the squeal of wheels just ahead of her on the bridge. Suddenly a car careened across the median and slammed into the railings. The railing gave way with a groan and scrape of metal. The car hung precariously, its undercarriage partly on the road and partly in midair. With another groan, the hood of the car dropped, but was held suspended by the broken and dislodged railing.

Sean was already picking up the radio to call for help as Lana grabbed her helmet and jumped out of the truck.

She reached the car and called. "Hang on. We're getting you some help."

A faint sound came from the front seat. "Help me."

"Can you move?"

"Yes."

"Try to come to the back of the car. We've got to get you out," Lana instructed calmly.

"I'll try."

Lana could see someone try to crawl over the seat. But with the movement, the car shifted again.

"Wait! Stop!"

Lana edged forward as close to the car as she could get.

"Lana, not too close. If that goes over, you'll go over with it," Sean's voice cautioned.

She turned to him. "If we don't do something, she's going over regardless."

"The eighty-second is on the way," Sean said, inspecting the car again.

Lana knew that the weight of the car would begin to pull on the guardrail and the car would fall. "We don't have time to wait."

"I've got rope in the truck."

"We don't have time, you'll have to hold my legs."

Sean looked grim but then nodded.

Lana yelled. "Can you open the driver's side window?"

She heard the sound of the window being lowered and a head emerged. "Stay there."

Lana got down on her stomach and moved closer to the edge of the bridge. Sean grabbed on to her ankles and braced himself against the concrete curb.

"Sean are you ready?"

"Yes," he said between clenched teeth. "Go."

She reached out into space, her stomach muscles straining. "Grab my hand. Hurry!"

"I don't know if you can hold me. I'm pregnant."

"Look, don't worry about us. Worry about grabbing my hand." The car groaned again and with a horrible scraping sound the car started to fall.

The woman reached out and Lana lunged for her hand.

Just as the car tumbled to the ground below, Lana grabbed for the woman. She felt as if her arm was being pulled from the socket, but she held on.

The woman struggled. "Stop moving. Try to hold still." The woman's terrified face looked up at her. "I know you're scared," Lana said, her heart pumping with determination and adrenaline, "but just hold on and stay still."

Lana slipped forward. She risked a glance back. Sean was holding them, but sweat was beginning to pop out on his forehead.

Suddenly, she felt herself slip forward again. When the woman jerked down, she screamed. Lana felt the woman's hand slip and she fought to hold on. Soon, motorists were helping Sean pull her and the woman to safety.

She heard the sirens of the fire engine and the ambulance trying to work through the traffic on the bridge.

As soon as the woman hit the ground, she said, "The baby's coming."

Lana checked her, while Sean ran for the ambulance. The head was already crowning and the woman was beginning to push. Lana stayed with her until the paramedics ran up, and Lana relinquished her spot just as the infant appeared.

Lana stood there for a moment, just stood there and watched the scene.

Sean, standing right behind her, as usual, asked, "Are you all right?"

She felt the tears start to well at the corners of her eyes.

"You all right, Dempsey?" the captain asked.

Sean looked at him. "She's fine. It's really me, Cap. I think I pulled something."

Lana couldn't stay one more minute. She walked away and heard the captain say, "Get to the hospital and take care of it. Have Dempsey drive you. We'll sort out things here."

She was standing at the railing to the bridge when Sean approached her, looking down at the wreckage and the sheer, terrible fall.

"Lana?"

"She had a little boy."

"I know."

Sean could sense that Lana's expression betrayed the horror of what might have happened had they not been there. He drew her over to the truck.

"I've been ordered to the hospital. I think I pulled a muscle in my shoulder."

"Get in. I'll drive," Lana said.

After an hour in the waiting room, Lana asked, "Do you want some coffee?" She was feeling edgy.

"Sure."

She got up, but the first thing she noticed was that

the nursery was on the fourth floor. Without thinking, she got into the elevator. As she exited, a nurse was coming out of the maternity room.

"Excuse me, Lana Dempsey from the eighty-second. There was a baby who was born on an overpass bridge just about an hour ago."

"Right. Ryan."

"Could you point him out?"

The nurse guided her over to the glass and searched the sleeping faces. "There he is. Third from the end."

"Is he okay?"

"He's fine. Are you the firefighter who saved his mother?"

Lana nodded. "Is she okay?"

"Also fine." The nurse touched her shoulder. "Good job."

Lana smiled softly and nodded again.

After a moment, the nurse left. Lana stared at the baby and felt tears forming again. When she'd started as a probie, she had this abstract notion about saving lives. It wasn't until her first rescue, that the abstract narrowed down to a real, specific person. She looked at Ryan's little pink face, his little bow of a mouth as tears slipped down her cheeks. He was why she got into firefighting.

Yet, the horrible fear of dropping the mother of this baby and being responsible for their deaths surged through her.

She'd mastered the ladder climbing, the tool skills, hose etiquette, ventilation, and ax wielding. She'd been burned, wet, dirty, and soot covered, but this emotional strain was something that she didn't know how to measure or how to train for. Each new experience left her a little more raw inside. This job demanded so much physically. Ah, but emotionally. How could you stow that?

What if she'd dropped the mother? Failed little Ryan. Those consequences were unbearable to think about.

She wiped at her tears and turned away. This rescue added even more scar tissue to an already broken heart.

BACK AT THE STATION HOUSE, Lana went immediately to the kitchen since it was her turn to cook.

Sean was close on her heels. "Are you sure you're up for this?"

"What? Cooking?"

"Staying. Maybe you should take some time."

"I'm fine. What about you?"

"It's only a slightly pulled muscle. I'll take some painkillers and it'll be fine. I'm just not supposed to hold on to two people dangling over a bridge anytime soon."

He stood there for a moment. "Are you sure you're all right?"

She rolled her shoulders because she didn't want to snap at Sean. "I was shaken up. That's all."

"Okay. I'll go get some other work done."

She wanted to call him back, but she couldn't look weak, not even in Sean's eyes. He was her best friend and now her lover, but she just couldn't let him know what had almost happened there on that bridge.

All her life, her father had told her not to show fear, don't let them see you're scared.

So she told Sean she was fine, even though he knew she wasn't. It seemed to damage their relationship every time it happened. A cut here, a chip there and it eroded and eroded. Working with a man you were sleeping with wasn't good, but working with a man you were sleeping with *and* who was your best friend was just plain stupid.

9

LANA SET THE FOOD on the table. Again, Pete took Sean's seat. When Sean came to the table, he sighed and took another chair.

But the minute she brought her food up to her mouth, the alarm sounded.

There were grumbles and groans as men threw down their napkins and headed to the engines.

The call came over the loudspeaker that the burning structure was a warehouse in the wharf district. As they pulled out of the fire station, the horn wailed warning motorists that Station 82 was entering the roadway.

When the engine pulled up, the structure was fully engaged.

"Don't bother going in," a firefighter said and Lana looked at him. The same guy from the other fires. Strong, square jaw with a ragged scar along the cheekbone. His turnout coat and pants looked almost brand-new. A probie? But if he was a probie, where was his veteran.

"Why?"

"We tried an interior attack, but the stairs collapsed. The whole roof is gonna come down,'' he explained.

Captain Troy nodded and said, ''Surround and drown people.''

Lana headed toward the specially-designed ladder with a hose attached, which was already being propelled into the air. Without missing a beat, she climbed up the seventy-five degree angled ladder, ascending through smoke and steam that obscured everything.

At the top of the eighty-foot ladder she took up the nozzle. She positioned it over the warehouse and opened the nozzle.

Water streamed out forcefully through a tip in a concentrated stream and then loosened and fell, like rippling ribbons of silver.

Lana found it peaceful at the top of the ladder, like sitting on a cloud in heaven watching hell burn. The wind picked up giving fuel to the fire and throwing a fine mist all around her. As time passed it soaked her through.

Once she started to shiver, she descended the ladder and Sean was waiting down at the bottom to take over.

For a moment he paused and swallowed.

''What's wrong?''

He turned to look at her, his eyes wide. ''Nothing.''

Without another word he scrambled up the ladder.

Lana watched him, making a mental note to ask him about it later.

Once there was nothing but smoldering ruins left of the warehouse, Lana began the tedious job of making sure that no living embers survived. All debris had to be pulled out and hosed down.

She walked toward the fire ground, but was brought up short.

"Don't even think about doing any snooping around in there." Bryant stood a few feet away from her, his helmet dangling from his hand. "Just do your scutt work and leave the investigation to me."

It took all the willpower she had not to snap back at him. "I'll do what my captain told me, but have you even looked at the reports?"

"No. I told you that you're off base. Those were basements. Of course there's going to be fuel type products in them."

"Bryant, you're…"

"Go ahead, Dempsey. Just give me a reason to write you up. I'd love some insubordination about right now."

"…incompetent," Sean finished for her. "Go ahead and write me up."

Bryant didn't even bother to glance at Sean. "Watch your step, Dempsey."

Brushing past Sean, he jammed his helmet on his head, cinched the strap beneath his chin, and headed into what was left of the building.

Lana turned to Sean. "How many times…"

"…do you have to tell me to mind my own business?" He pulled off his glove and tilted her chin up. "I'm going to stick up for you because it's in my nature to do so. If you don't like it, that's too bad, Dempsey." Sean walked past her and entered the building to haul out more debris.

Lana's irritation with him dissipated. It was strange to see this part of Sean.

She entered the building and watched Bryant half-heartedly poke around the debris. She never once saw him take any soil samples or check any of the concrete. He looked in her direction and she quickly looked away. Inside she was waging a fierce battle. She had to keep her record clean if she was going to become captain. If she so much as took a soil sample to test it and Bryant found out, she'd get reprimanded for sure. But how could she let a potential arsonist get away with destroying property and risking lives and do nothing?

The answer was simple. She couldn't.

BACK AT THE STATION, after her shower, Lana stayed up in the bunkroom while her squad members reheated the lasagna and had a meal. She dialed up Sienna, who answered on the first ring.

"Sienna, it's Lana."

"Hey, good to hear from you. I've been meaning

to call. How goes it with Sean? Did the apology work out?''

Sienna's concern made Lana's heart tight. ''Yes, it did. Thanks for your advice. Listen, I need you to do something for me.''

''What?''

''A background check?''

''Unofficially?'' Sienna asked, her tone expressionless.

Lana closed her eyes, thinking about the chance she was taking. But she couldn't ignore her conscience and avoid looking at herself in a mirror every day. If she did nothing about her suspicions and someone died because of it, she'd never forgive herself. ''Yes, because if it gets out I'm doing this, my career is toast.''

''Who is it?''

''Dane Bryant.''

Sienna gasped. ''Bryant! Are you crazy? You're career will be *burnt toast* if he gets wind you're looking into his background.''

''Can you do it discreetly?''

''Yes, you know I will. One of your hunches is worth two of mine.''

After disconnecting from Sienna, she went downstairs, got herself some food and sat down at the table next to Sean. She wasn't really hungry, but she didn't want her squad members to notice she was acting any differently.

Sean got up a few minutes later to get more bread.

Pete Meadows took Sean's vacated seat, and sat just a little bit too close. He scooted Sean's dish over.

She gave him a weak smile and shifted her chair over to give herself more room.

"That was quite a save you had this afternoon at the bridge."

The roll that Lana had taken a bite of dissolved to ashes in her mouth. Without looking at Pete, she nodded.

"I heard the drop was eighty feet. Would have killed her and the baby, too."

Lana's stomach knotted and she toyed with the lasagna on her plate, nodding again.

"I saw Bryant giving you a hard time again. That guy needs to embrace affirmative action."

Lana was thankful that Pete changed topics. "What do you know about him, Pete?"

"He and I were on the same squad before he got a job with arson. He couldn't cut it as a firefighter. If you ask me, that's why he moved on."

"Meadows, you're in my seat."

Lana looked up to see Sean standing behind Pete's chair.

"There are plenty of seats, O'Neill."

"But I was sitting here."

All conversation at the table stopped at the note in Sean's voice. Pete looked at Lana, surprise in his eyes. Easygoing, never-have-a-problem-O'Neill was making a scene.

"You've never objected before."

"I am now. Move."

Pete picked up his plate and glass and gave up Sean's seat. Sean sat down and started eating without a care in the world. All around the table there were smirks and wry smiles.

Lana had to bite her lip to keep from grabbing him and planting a kiss on his attractive mouth. His forceful attitude stirred something inside her, made her juices start to flow. Made her feel reckless.

Sean slanted her a look as if sensing her arousal. She could feel the heat of his gaze against the side of her face. When she looked at him, his eyes blazed with a deep awareness that made her knees weak.

Too bad they were on duty.

She only jumped slightly when his left hand landed on her thigh, massaging gently. He continued to eat all the while his fingers moved up and down her leg, giving her goose bumps, wishing it wasn't another thirty-two hours before they were off duty.

They had no more calls that night and Lana went up the stairs to the bunkroom. She thought it was empty until she sensed Sean's presence.

Lana clutched Sean's shoulders, as he pinned her to the wall and seared his hot, wet mouth on hers.

Winding a handful of her hair around his hand, he tilted her head back covering her mouth with a kiss that was meant to inflame, to detonate, to ravage, and Lana groaned softly. He seemed to absorb the sound, drawing his hands up her torso.

Lana lost it. Grappling for every breath, she savored his succulent mouth, drawing his tongue deeper into hers.

He cupped her face. The feel of his hands made her whole body tremble. Sobbing against his mouth, she reached down and dragged her fingers up the thick, hard ridge under his zipper and molded her hand over the hard bulge. Sean tugged her hand away, making a rough sound deep in his throat. Stretching his arms around her neck, he softened the kiss; then, breathing hard, he pulled away from her mouth, taking control.

''I know what you need,'' he said softly.

Lana's senses overloaded when he dragged her against him, the feel of him thick and hard and fully aroused at the juncture of her thighs driving the breath from her. Grasping the back of her head, he covered her mouth with another searing kiss, his heart hammering against her. His hands slipped down her body to her hips. Tightening his hold, he wedged his knee between her legs, and Lana fought for breath as he settled heavily between her thighs.

Drawing up her leg, she tried to cup him, but Sean grabbed her wrist, forcing her hand away.

''This time is for you.''

Sean held her still against him, brushing his

mouth against hers with excruciating slowness. Lana wanted desperately to move against him and force his mouth down harder on hers, but he resisted. His mouth barely touching hers, he ran his tongue along her bottom lip. "Sweet. Very sweet."

He deepened the kiss, then slowly, so slowly, flexed his hips against hers, aligning his arousal tightly with her pelvis. Lana sobbed against his mouth, thrusting her hips to increase the pressure.

"Easy does it," he whispered unevenly. He kissed her again, his mouth wonderfully tormenting.

He undid her pants and slid one hand under the elastic of her panties going to the hot, moist core of her that ached for his touch.

Feeling as if she was drowning in the deep, vital sensations, Lana shuddered and turned her face against him as he slid his fingers over her straining core, his touch turning her weak.

Dragging her mouth away, she shuddered and turned her head against his, the muscles in her back bunching as she flexed her hips against his hand. His lips moved from her mouth to her neck, trailing kisses to the hollow behind her ear, and then he returned to her mouth, kissing her with a thoroughness that went on and on and on.

Using his thumb to continue with the sensual torment on her aching, sensitized bud, he thrust two fingers into her.

It was too much. Lana cried out his name on a

whisper and arched against him, her body bowing, arching as she clutched at his shoulders and raised her hips. Sean thrust again into her swollen, wet heat. Her whole body went rigid as he thrust while he worked her moist center.

Lana came apart in his arms, the tension coming together into one piercing center. With one urgent thrust, her center ignited, and tremors shivered through her. Sean covered her mouth, taking her cry into him, effectively muffling it.

Lana clung to him and buried her face against his neck, feeling as if she'd shattered into a million brilliant pieces.

Sean adjusted his hold; his hand splayed wide at the back of her head, holding her with such absolute tenderness that it made her throat close up. Gently, he adjusted her clothing and held her for a long time, until they heard footsteps on the stairs.

Then reluctantly, he let her go.

IN HER BUNK THAT NIGHT Lana couldn't help glancing over at Sean sleeping deeply as if he'd been the one who had the explosive orgasm. She wished she could go over there and curl up with him.

As it was, there were no calls that night. But that didn't stop Lana from having broken sleep as she tossed and turned. When she woke in the morning to face the rest of her shift, she struggled up out of a nightmare. One where, instead of the pregnant woman looking up at her with a panicked look in her eyes, it'd been her father. But her dream had gone very differently.

She'd dropped him.

THE DREAM SEEMED TO HAUNT her as she moved through her shift, taking a call for a car accident that required the driver to be cut out with the jaws of life, a water rescue down at the pier, a man entangled in power lines that fell while he was cutting a tree, and laughingly, a cat caught on a roof.

At the end of the shift, almost everyone had left while Lana put her gear into her locker. The alarm sounded and effectively emptied the firehouse of the oncoming crew. Lana walked toward the stairs when Sean grabbed her arm and pulled her into the closet where they kept the extra SCBAs.

"What are you doing?" Lana said softly.

"I can't wait for a bed," he said, taking Lana's mouth like a man who was starving.

He pressed her against the ladder, knowing that even a week ago, he wouldn't have thought about having Lana like this in a place where they could be discovered. He would have fantasized about it, but he wouldn't have done it. When he realized that Lana thought he wouldn't mind about the souvenir, he'd finally had enough of complacency. It fueled this change in him and made him want to take the kinds of chances he'd never have taken before. Taking his life, including his love life to new heights. But only with Lana. Now, he didn't care, he was sick of being everyone's best friend, always there to help out. He wanted to take something for himself, be stronger and tougher. The thought of that lent an air of excitement to his already aroused flesh.

"I really like this side of you, Sean. It makes me hot."

"You bring it out in me. I can't seem to care about anything but you."

"I think about you, the desire in your eyes, the way you look at me. It makes me feel cherished, wanted, needed."

"I do need you, want you, cherish you." His mouth slammed down on hers. Her reaction sizzled through him as her tongue demanded entrance and he opened for her. A groan escaped him when she teased the roof of his mouth, the inside of his upper lip.

He went wild when she bit his bottom lip. But this was his fantasy and he was going to force her to do what he wanted. "Touch my cock, Lana."

She didn't hesitate as she undid the button of his jeans and pulled the zipper down. She took his erection into her hands and bent down to run her tongue along his hardness.

It turned him on that Lana was so receptive to this dark side of him.

He gasped and his body strained upward. "Take me in your mouth."

With a soft moan she slid her moist lips over him, working her mouth up and down his arousal until the heavy sensations threatened to overwhelm him.

"No more Lana or I'll come," he said fiercely and dragged her against him, covering her mouth in a searing kiss.

Sean had taken her by surprise. He'd changed right before her eyes and it was the kind of man she'd always craved, knew that this dark side of Sean lurked inside of him. Had she seen it in his eyes? Had she known all along all she had to do was take him into her body to unleash it? She found that she could let her control go with him. Although experiencing a volatile mix of fear and pleasure, she knew deep down in her heart that she could trust him.

The moment Sean's hand wrapped around the back of her neck and his tongue surged into her mouth, she was lost again.

Lana moved restlessly against him. She roughly pushed him back so he was flush against the closet door. He guided her hands back down to his erection. With his hands over hers, he rubbed her palms along his arousal.

"Is this what you want, Lana?"

She opened herself to him, body and soul. Just as he'd fantasized, but he hadn't expected his domination to feel so good, had no idea that this side of him had lurked inside until Lana had brought it out of him. When she'd seduced him, she'd changed their relationship into something more beautiful than he could have imagined.

There was something in his voice, something dark and delicious that sent heat to the core of her, escalating her need until she felt taut as a bowstring. Strong desire coursed through her, demanding consummation, an urgent, primal need her body had to join with his.

"Yes." The word came out on a breath of air. She stroked his hair, drawing his mouth back to her.

The feel of her ravenous lips wiped out any last vestiges of thought Sean had. He slanted his arm across her lower torso, turning her so that her back was now against the door.

He pushed and pulled at her clothes, stripping her down to nothing in a matter of minutes. She did the same for him. With a soft groan, he entered her, lifting her up and against the door as his hips moved in rapid-fire thrusts.

Lana cupped the back of his neck and held on to him as if he was an anchor in a violent storm.

He pushed away from the door holding her against him with sheer muscle and sinew. Lana moved against him sure of his power and support.

He backed her toward the ladder to the roof. "Grab on," he said hoarsely.

Lana turned to look and released her fingers from around his neck. She grasped a rung and Sean stretched her out as he thrust into her, watching the erotic movement of her breasts, the fine sheen of perspiration that covered her body, the pleasure that played across her expressive and beautiful face.

Unbearably aroused by his stare and the dark fire in his eyes, she'd never been this open with a man. Her chest rose and fell, her breathing uneven and quick. He groaned as he felt the slickness of her sheath. She saw Sean's nostrils flare, watched him touch his tongue to his lips as though tasting her scent.

Sensation after sensation poured through her in unbearable waves of charged pleasure. Low in her belly, pressure built like a coiled spring ratcheting tighter and tighter. The sheer pleasure on Sean's face dragged a moan out of her. He was gorgeous, each muscle in his chest delineated, sweat rolling down over the taut muscles in little rivulets. His biceps, coiled curves of solid power, supported her weight. His hair was damp and clinging to his temples. Her gaze connected with his as if drawn into an embrace. It was as if he touched her soul and she touched his.

He slid his hand up her body over the indentation of her hip, the swell of her stomach. Moving forward, his eyes glued to hers, he pressed her back against the ladder. Leaning in, he kissed her mouth with a deepness that seemed to go to the very bottom of her being, turning her inside out and upside down. The very unfolding of her soul like a flower opening to the power of the sun.

She got lost in the well of his gaze and fell and fell and fell, but instead of a searing jolt at the bottom, there was comfort and joy, and buoyancy that lifted her up and up and up, holding her in a cherished warmth.

She loved him beyond time and space and anything that could be defined. Truly, deeply, the man of her dreams, the man she was destined to hold and treasure.

Her heart twisted inside her with excruciating pain. She knew all this and yet, she still had to let him go. She couldn't have both her job and him. It wasn't going to work. But until it became an issue, she would cherish each moment she had with him. When she let him go, it would be for good.

"Sean," she said in the still air of the enclosed closet. In supplication, she rubbed her face against his, reveling in the feel of his skin, in the commanding movement of his body deep inside her. With a silent plea, she grasped a higher rung and raised her body offering, giving, beseeching.

He bowed toward her, closing his eyes, breathing hard. He moved against her, the heat of him, the feel of him sliding in and out of her, electric.

Lana sobbed out his name on a rasping moan,

arching into him, her body jerking and convulsing, heat and sensation that she'd never experienced before. She reached for him with her body, straining against, trying to hold on to the highly charged, erotic moment.

By focusing all her awareness on the smooth motion of their bodies heightened the thrill.

"Don't close your eyes," he whispered, thrusting hard into her. "Look at what I'm doing to you. Feel my body take yours. Thrust into you, deep into you. Watch."

With a slow, hard push he made her watch as he moved in and out of her. "I want to watch you watching me." He reached down between their bodies and touched her hot aching core catapulting her to the most shattering climax of her life. The entire time she pulsed around him, Sean didn't take his eyes off her face. And when he felt her go slack, he continued to stare at her and hold her gaze while he thrust his hips harder and harder, pumping until his body jackknifed and it was her turn to watch the hard sensations take him into his own breathtaking orgasm.

10

THEY HEADED FOR HIS APARTMENT because it was closer, stopping only long enough to get food. Once in his place they ate ravenously, shed their clothes and made love in his big bed just as ravenously.

Exhausted from the shift and drained by lovemaking, they fell asleep in each other's arms.

Lana jerked from sleep, the sound of Sean's name echoing in her head. That stupid, damn dream of the woman dangling from the bridge again, only this time it'd been Sean hanging between life and death.

And she'd dropped him. Watched as his terrified face grew smaller and smaller.

Drawn in spite of her fears, she knew what that dream meant. It didn't take a psychiatrist to tell her that she didn't want to fail him.

She turned her head on the pillow and gazed at him sprawled easily and accommodatingly on only one side of the bed.

Firefighters could sleep anywhere, she thought, even a small cramped space, a space Sean would no doubt give up to her. His generous nature couldn't be disputed. Even with this new side of him, he continued to give of himself unerringly.

He was deeply asleep, facedown on his stomach so that his premium backside was peeking from the covers along with one sleek hip. And she all of a sudden and quite terrifyingly had to fight the fact that she was starting to think of exclusivity with him. It wasn't something they had talked about, but she saw his reaction whenever Pete got close to her. Thinking of Sean with another woman made the little green-eyed monster bite hard on her heart.

His hair was tousled, thick and drew her hand to smooth it from his temple. The skin on his chest she knew was silky because she'd had it pressed against her breasts. And she marveled how she wanted him again.

The shattering way he made love to her was addictive and she couldn't imagine ever letting another man touch her like she let Sean touch her.

She wanted him.

All of him.

She wanted to absorb him into her, let him fill up and shore up all those places where she lacked. Good and bad, physical and emotional, soul and heart. She wanted every bit of him.

And knew with trepidation that she probably always had. That he was the man her heart had no doubt been daydreaming of for years, this generous

man who was becoming someone she found irre-
sistible.

He was the man her spirit had been looking for.

As fascinated by the recognition, as she hungered
for it, she moved closer to him to get a better view
of the man every part of her longed for.

She couldn't imagine getting along without his
friendship.

Didn't want to.

She needed him.

And that made him dangerous.

She waited for the irrational fear, the customary
rush of apprehension, to put distance between her
and the thought. It didn't and that was a little sweet
surprise.

He opened his sleepy smoky-gray eyes. Smiling
with a dangerous languor, he touched the skin of her
cheek, rubbing his thumb along the indentation.

"Hi."

"Hi, yourself."

"You're still here."

"Where else do you think I'd rather be?"

"I don't know. Independent Lana." He moved
closer to her, drawing her into his arms. "Intimacy
and independence are sometimes like oil and water.
They don't mix. Giving yourself over physically is
so easy. Trusting someone in slumber when you are
your most vulnerable can be more difficult."

"I like sleeping with you, Sean, and seeing your face first thing after I open my eyes."

"Thank you," he whispered.

"For what?"

"For letting me have that." He unfolded, caressed her cheek, her jaw. Ran a gentle thumb across her lips so that they parted slightly, readily and tried to follow when he drew his hand away. "For giving me that kind of depth in our friendship."

"We've been friends a long time."

"But we haven't been lovers that long." Sean offered her a purely male, purely wicked grin.

"It's been wonderful."

He nodded. "So now that we've established that we trust each other, why don't you tell me what keeps you tossing and turning both at the station and here?"

Lana bit her lip and should have realized that Sean would know that although she acted fine, she was a chaotic mess inside. "It's just that for a split second, I almost dropped her."

Sean didn't miss a beat. "But you didn't."

"I know."

"Why are you dwelling on this?"

"I don't know. I'm just sure that if I had lost her I wouldn't have been able to forgive myself, especially after I saw the baby. He was so little."

"You've got to let this go."

"I know."

"Second-guessing yourself and replaying these incidents with a different outcome only makes it worse."

"You're right. I know that you're right. Except when I dream, I dream that I'm dropping my father...and you."

"I understand you don't want to fail me, but what's up with your dad?"

"He wants me to make captain," she whispered.

Sean was silent for a moment. He shifted and moved closer to her. "At Station 82?"

His hand went to her hair and he slowly caressed her as she answered. "Yes, you know it's his old station and tradition."

"You're afraid of failing at that?"

She snuggled closer to him, sighing. "I guess deep down inside I must be."

"Are you feeling that maybe this dream you have doesn't stem from what you want, but what he wants?"

"What do you mean?"

For a moment Sean didn't answer, then he said, "How long has he been pushing you?"

Lana felt the bedrock of their relationship crack with a very fine fissure. "You mean helping me?"

"If that's what you want to call it."

"That's what it is. I've had this dream of becoming captain ever since I could remember."

"Why didn't you ever mention it before?"

Lana felt something shift inside her and she shied away from it. It was too big for her to contemplate, too big for her to deal with.

"The subject never came up," she said steadfastly with pure conviction in her voice.

"That sounds like bull to me. Maybe you're not as sure as you think you are."

"I'm sure," she insisted. But inside she was panicking. Why? She *was* sure it was what she wanted.

Sean's skeptical eyes seemed to look right through her. She didn't have anything to hide, did she?

"If that's the case, we'll have to think about this."

"Why?" she asked, her voice gruff and uneven.

Sliding his arms around her back, he hugged her hard. "Lana, I can't stay at the eighty-second if you're appointed as captain there."

Lana closed her eyes and hugged him back "Why do we have to talk about this now?"

Sean shifted his hold. Spanning her jaw with his hand, he tipped her face up and brushed a soft, reassuring kiss against her mouth. "You think our relationship won't be long-term?"

Her head lifted and her voice was steady, husky. "I didn't say that, but I think you're jumping the gun."

"I'll have to transfer. It's the only answer."

"I think we can deal with this in the future, when we have to, Sean."

Sean was quiet. "All right. I'll drop it for now."

Lana felt a moment of unease and it made her close her eyes. She liked this new side of Sean, but the assertiveness that went with it was annoying, making her question something she'd believed in all her life.

LANA SAT OUTSIDE THE TESTING office looking at the people going in and coming out. She had to register if she was going to take the test, but Sean's words echoed in her head. Was this something that she really wanted? Of course it was. She'd worked hard and long for it every day of her life up to this very moment.

Yet, she just sat there and stared.

From the time she could remember, she wanted to be a firefighter like her father and not only excel at the job but reach the goal of captain.

The other odd thing about this captain business was that she hadn't said a word to Sean about this test. She hadn't told anyone except Sienna and Kate. Next to them Sean was her best friend, and this morning had been the perfect opportunity to tell him she'd been studying for it. So why hadn't she?

Finally, she headed toward the office, but it felt as if she were going to her doom.

LANA PLOPPED HERSELF DOWN in the chair across from Sienna's desk.

Sienna smiled. "You look good, positively glowing. Sean?"

Lana couldn't help but grin back. "I'd say he's positively glowing, too."

"So the dare worked for you, too?"

"I guess it did, sort of."

"Why do you say that?"

"I told Sean about wanting to become captain."

"And?"

"He questioned whether it was my dream or my father's."

"Why would he say that?"

"I saved a woman from falling two days ago."

"Saw that on the news."

"I almost dropped her, Sienna."

"Wow. How have you been handling it?"

"You know how this job is. It's ninety-nine percent mental. Getting through each call is mind over matter. That's where the control freak thing comes into play."

"Right. Good old control."

"Anyway, I had this dream about dropping my dad. I told Sean. He thinks it's because I don't want to fail him. When I told him about the captain's goal, he thought maybe it's my dad's dream and not my own. That's why I'm dreaming about dropping him."

"Is it?"

"No!" Lana said more sharply than she meant to.

Sienna raised her brows. "Have you signed up for the test?"

"Yes. I did. So see. I'm committed."

"That proves it. Lana, I've never known you to go forward with something you don't feel one hundred percent about. You must want this very badly. Look what you've accomplished to get where you are now."

"Right. You're right. I'm second-guessing myself for nothing."

Sienna nodded. "So do you want to know what I found out about Bryant?"

"Sure."

"Nothing."

"Not even a speeding ticket?"

"Nope. He's clean as a whistle, except..." Sienna said, looking up at Lana.

"What?"

"He's received some extra money lately. Two payments."

"Bribes?"

Sienna shrugged. "Not sure. Could be anything— extra work, inheritance, or lottery winnings. Problem is that unless he's a suspect, I can't go further with an investigation."

"I'm probably off base about this guy anyway.

Incompetence isn't a crime. He just doesn't do his job well.''

"You think he might be the arsonist?"

"I thought so, but it could be because I really dislike him."

"Could be."

"Pete Meadows said he was also incompetent as a firefighter, so I'm probably wrong."

"That leaves a suspect out there somewhere."

"Right. Someone is setting those fires."

"Did you get a soil sample from the last one?"

"No. If I get caught doing that, the captain will come down on me hard."

"How about I do it?"

Lana sat up in her chair. "Good idea and that leaves me out of it."

"I'll let you know the results."

"The results of what?"

Lana's head whipped around and Bryant was standing next to Sienna's desk.

For a moment she just stared at him, then came to her senses. She stood up and slid the folder with the results of Bryant's background check under some of Sienna's other folders. "It was personal, Lieutenant Bryant."

He glared at her, but she was pretty sure that he hadn't seen the folder. If he had he wouldn't have hesitated to make a stink about it and rat her out to her captain.

"I'll see you later, Sienna."

Sienna nodded and Lana headed to her car, relieved that Bryant had been too distracted by sneering at her.

She still had her dry cleaning to pick up before she could go back to Sean's and snuggle with him.

Lana got into her car swinging her purse onto the seat. She dislodged the folder that Tim the photographer had given her at Bryant's office. The pictures inside scattered in a fanning array across the floorboard of her car.

The mysterious firefighter was in each picture.

11

LANA FELT IN HER BONES that this was a break-through. Something concrete that she could show her captain and Bryant. They would have to acknowledge it.

But what if she did give the information to Bryant and he botched it or worse yet, still wouldn't believe her. He could damage the case. That was something she couldn't allow. It was up to her to find out who this guy was.

She stuffed the photos back in the manila folder, deciding that she was going to keep quiet about it until she had a name and some more evidence.

She put the car in gear and drove over to Sean's apartment. When she walked through the door, he was sitting at his breakfast bar reading the paper.

"Hi, babe," he said, returning the kiss she gave him as she approached.

"Where have you been?"

"Out on errands," she hedged, deliberately keeping the information about the test registration to herself along with the photos.

Sean would tell her to turn them into Bryant and

leave the investigation alone. He would caution her that if she was really serious about becoming captain, a dark mark on her record could jeopardize her dream. So, maybe she wasn't as committed as she thought she was.

Well, he would be wrong, she thought as she stole a piece of toast off his plate. She was committed. It was that the investigation was so important. Yeah, that's it. The thrill she got from pitting her mind against a criminal fire starter had nothing to do with her decision to pursue the case alone and in secret.

She grabbed a cup of coffee and said, "Let's go out on the balcony and relax."

"No."

His sharp answer made her remember how he'd hesitated going up the ladder at the warehouse fire. "Sean, I've never seen you on your balcony. Why?"

"It's too windy."

"There's no wind today."

"I don't like the bugs."

"I don't think you'd get many bugs this high up."

"I don't have comfortable chairs out there."

"Sean, are you afraid of heights?"

His face colored and he looked away, "No." He put the paper up to his face.

"You are," she said, grabbing the paper away from him and meeting his darting eyes.

"You were afraid to go up the ladder, but I've seen you walk across a steel girder to fight a fire."

"Okay, so I'm afraid of heights. It's something that I do because the job requires it. Doesn't mean I have to like it or succumb to my fear."

"Jeez, I can't believe this. I had no idea."

"Sometimes it gets the best of me."

"Sean, you live on the twenty-third floor. Why is that?"

"Defiance."

"You helped me put up my wallpaper."

"The trick is not to look down."

"I can't believe you never told me this." She felt a large dose of guilt, thinking about what she was keeping from him.

"A guy has to have some secrets."

"I guess he does."

His eyes shifted to the folder in her hands. "What's that?"

"So, I guess we'll have to move your mattress to the floor," she teased.

"Why?" he said.

She smiled, shoving the folder with the photos deeper into her bag.

"I wouldn't want you to be up too high to make love to me."

He smiled wickedly. "I said the trick was not to look down. I think I can handle it."

He grabbed her around the waist and dragged her into his room.

Afterward, Lana wandered back out to the kitchen to make a pot of tea. She picked up the paper and scanned the headlines. A story snagged her attention. Condo developer William Morrison had purchased the properties where the second and third fires had occurred.

LATER THAT DAY SHE MADE the rounds and asked at each of the fire stations around the area of each arson, but no one knew the mysterious firefighter in the photo.

When she pulled up to her house, she saw that Sean was sitting on her porch rocking in one of her chairs.

She approached, her heart in her throat at how good he looked.

"Hey."

He smiled and stood, meeting her at the stairs. He gave her a kiss. "I've been thinking that it's finally time that I overcome this fear of heights."

"Oh, you have. How?"

"Go climbing."

"Where?"

"I'll show you."

SEAN SAT in his parked car on an overlook jutting from the San Francisco hills, adjacent to the Golden

Gate Bridge. He left a sleeping Lana in his car to get an unobstructed view of the bridge.

The same old apprehension he'd always felt gnawed at him as they'd traversed the 480 miles to San Francisco. It was time for him to face this fear and overcome it. A fear that had grown out of a need to prove himself. Maybe that was why he was always doing everything his family wanted. Live up to his parents' expectations that he was a good man and a contributing citizen. He was sure now that was why he became a firefighter. To make his parents proud of him, but now he wanted to be proud of himself.

In Lana's arms, he'd discovered that the only expectations he had to live up to were his own.

"So this is why you refused to tell me where we were going and I had to pack a bag. The Golden Gate Bridge?" Lana said in a sleepy voice as she came up behind him.

"Lots of firefighters climb it," Sean replied, standing shoulder to shoulder with her.

"I know, but are you sure of your reasons for climbing it?" Lana challenged.

"Yes. I want to overcome my fear of heights."

"You've been thinking about this since we talked."

"I've been thinking about a lot of things since we talked," he said. "Mostly about how I always do what I'm asked regardless of whether I want to or not.''

"Like?''

"Like how I never stepped on anyone's toes and always ate my vegetables.''

"Do you mean the reputation you have of being a nice guy?''

"Yes. I'm sick of that.''

"It was a good start when you asked Pete to move out of your seat.''

Without replying to her words, he began to walk to the bridge. Lana followed him.

When they reached the suspension part of the bridge, Lana grabbed his arm. "Sean, you don't have to prove anything to me.''

"Why do you think this has to do with you? I need to prove to myself that I'm the kind of man who can take risks and live up to my own expectations.''

"I just want to make sure, that's all. I didn't know that you were afraid of heights. Now you want to scale the Golden Gate. You don't have to.''

"It's true, Lana, that I wouldn't want to be seen as a coward in your eyes.''

"Sean…''

"Wait, I'm not finished. I need to do this for me. To prove something to myself.''

"Just so you know, I won't think any less of you

if you walk back to the car and we go get something to eat.''

He nodded. She cupped his face and held it between her hands. "You're awesome. I've always thought so, before you changed, after you changed. It doesn't matter to me.''

"So, are you going?''

"I've followed you through flaming walls of fire. What makes you think that I wouldn't go on this journey with you?''

"Your amazing intellect?''

"This isn't about intellect. This is about a rite of passage. Your rite of passage. I'm along for the ride.''

He smiled and pulled her close for a quick embrace. One after the other, they stepped onto the suspension cable.

They moved along carefully, Lana a warm, distinct presence behind him. The three-foot-in-diameter cable they walked on was now 320 feet into the air. On either side of them, a thin wire reached all the way up to the north tower that was their objective.

When Sean reached the top, he turned to look at her. Her hair blew in the wind, tiny wisps around her face. Her eyes were shining.

"It's beautiful," he said.

"Sure, if you overlook the death spiral of a fall,

the wind whipping us around and the fact that I'm starving,'' she said close to his ear.

Chuckling, Sean looked down into her face. She was a piece of work, all right. Insecure and tough, feisty and afraid, fierce and full of bluff, altogether amazing and astounding, breathtaking and absolutely beautiful.

All at once laughter faded. Because in a little more than a few days he'd discovered that he liked being a bit reckless. It astonished him, and if he'd been smart it should have scared him.

For better or worse, though, all it did was make him feel more human and more powerful, more… himself than he'd ever felt in his life.

It was then that he knew he loved her. Not for any other reason than because she was Lana. His heart jolted in his chest unsure of what he should do with these feelings he had. Should he tell her or not?

He decided not to. It wasn't the time or the place. He looked over to the east at the San Francisco skyline in the distance, framed by the long graceful cables. The familiar feeling of fear wasn't there. It wasn't there when he turned his head to study the island of the notorious prison Alcatraz, lit up to look like a small castle. He looked down from the dizzying height and saw the surf roll against the cliffs, mingling with the wind to make a soft hissing sound.

The international orange of the bridge took on a dark muted ginger hue at night. Soothing and comforting.

"Hey, are we going to stay up here all night?"

"I could."

Lana smiled and looked around. "I don't see any place to eat around here, O'Neill and as I said, I'm hungry," she groused.

They made their way down the suspension. "So was that some kind of male bonding thing we just experienced?" Lana asked.

"There is nothing male about you, Lana."

"You know what I mean."

"I know what you mean and yeah, we bonded." He wouldn't trade this night for anything in his life. He looked up at the North Tower and smiled. He'd mastered his fear and it made his chest tight to know that Lana had been there to share the experience with him.

He discovered quite a bit about her, about himself and what he cherished in his life.

AFTER GETTING A BITE, they got a room at a nearby hotel. Tired, Sean had fallen asleep, but woke from a light doze when the shower began. He got up and silently opened the bathroom door. The shower had one of those see-through shower curtains and he stood there in the bathroom, his back against the door and watched Lana.

Her body was tight and toned, flowing lines of hard female curves. His hands tingled as he stared at her plump, luscious breasts crowned with rich mocha-colored nipples. Nipples he'd rolled between his fingers, flushed and hard against his tongue, his hungry, suckling mouth.

The sheerness of the shower curtain guaranteed him a spectacular view of her soft, rounded thighs, the creamy globes of her ass, and the enticing divide between them.

She arched her back and leaned her head back to wet her hair, thrusting her breasts out. He put his hands in his pockets, shifting against the door.

She soaped her hair and used her fingers to rinse it, sensually drawing them through the heavy, wet mass. She sighed softly, a sound that cut through him like a knife.

She picked up a bar of soap and drew it slowly down her arms, over her shoulders and neck. Water and soap mingled as she used the flat of her hand to massage the creamy bubbles into a lather against her even creamier skin.

She cupped her breasts and slid the soap across her nipples and they tightened and distended. Dragging the bar down her stomach, she stopped just shy of her mound. With one hand she moved the shower curtain aside. "Want to wash my back, O'Neill?"

He walked to the shower and said, "Tease," as he stripped off his bottoms and grabbed a condom from the counter. He stepped into the charged air of the shower. He liked Lana naked and wet, it reminded him of the excitement the first time they'd made love and he wanted to relive it.

She took the latex and sheathed him before pressing her lips to his. He sank into her, into the slickness of her mouth. His hands cupped her bottom and drew her against him.

Sean's head dipped down to her warm velvet tipped breasts and took the hardened peaks into his mouth in turn as he lifted her off her feet and set her against the wall. Lana supported herself on his shoulders as he deftly guided her onto his hard cock.

She gasped in gratification at the sweet feel of him stretching her with his pulsating flesh. Bracing her against the warmed tiles of the shower, he slowly pumped his hips, easing in and out with slow seductive strokes.

Lana cried out her satisfaction. His movements intensified, thrusting deeply into her as if he wanted to climb inside and lose himself in her. The sweet pulsations of Lana's climax sent him into his own and he moaned against her moist, clean-smelling skin at the powerful release.

He slipped out of her and pulled her against him, letting her ride slowly down his body until her face was level with his own. Her hands kneaded the bunched muscles of his biceps as she leaned against him weakly.

He moved finally, drying them off and getting into bed. Releasing an unsteady sigh, he gathered her up in a secure embrace, tucking her head against the curve of his neck. He didn't say anything. He just closed his eyes and drew her deeper into his embrace, his chest tightening.

Lana started to stroke him, but he caught her hand and lifted it to his mouth, then held it immobile against his chest. He waited until she relaxed in his arms, then he adjusted his hold. He wanted to connect with her, but not only in the physical sense.

"Do you remember the time we had the ladder climbing competition when we were at the academy?"

She didn't say anything for the longest time; then he felt her smile. "You mean the one where I beat your ass?"

He nodded and stroked her temple, "Yeah, two times."

"That's right."

He smiled and stared into the darkness, remembering. "You looked at me with that smug little expression, like you could conquer the world."

She laughed softly and adjusted her head on his shoulder. "What I remember is that you had that same smug look on your face."

"I had to feign bravado. It was all I had at the time."

There was a brief pause, one that was underscored

with reminiscence; then she spoke, her voice soft. "Oh, Sean. I had no idea."

"Of course you didn't. I didn't tell anyone. I wanted to be a firefighter more than anything, but at that moment I was scared to death of climbing that ladder. I didn't know how I was going to do it."

Another recollection filtered through the others, a very special recollection, and he smiled a little, the details still crystal clear in his mind. He tightened his arm around her hip in an attention-getting hug. "Lana?"

"Hmm?"

He smoothed the thick fall of hair from her face. "Your challenge got me up the ladder."

"But I still beat you."

"Soundly."

Her voice was laced with amusement when she responded. "You were so good at everything else. I wanted to get your attention."

Sean grinned and gave her hip a little pinch. "You had my attention. I have to say I was pretty skeptical of a woman on the squad, but you and your classmates proved me wrong."

"That wasn't the attention I was talking about."

"No?"

"You know it. I never stood a chance against all that virility and charm."

He gave her another little pinch, and she caught

his hand, dragging his arms around her waist. He drew her closer, absently rubbing his stubbled chin against her hair. ''I also remember that you were quite the flirt.'' He drew her even closer, brushing a soft, sensual kiss against her ear. ''Remember?''

A shiver coursed through her, and she turned her head toward his caress, her voice weak and breathless when she responded. ''I wanted you even then.''

''We came close.''

''Yes. I remember.''

He'd never forget it. They had just graduated and a party was in full swing at Mahoney's. They had danced a sultry number, the lights in the bar were dim and most of the celebrants were drunk, including them. His arms had been around her, her pressed up tight to his body and he hadn't been able to hide anything from her. He recalled how beautiful she looked with her loose hair and dark eyes. He'd bent his head and then that voice had kicked in. It told him that kissing Lana would be a mistake. That lovers never lasted, but friendship was for a lifetime. Even in his stupor he knew that he wanted Lana in his life for a very long time. Jeopardizing what they had just wasn't worth it.

The memory of how close he'd come to her lips turned his pulse thick and heavy, and he closed his eyes and trailed his mouth across her ear and down her neck, his breathing suddenly erratic. Lana whispered his name and moved into his arms, and on a deep slow kiss, the darkness closed in around them. And he refused to let his anxiety matter right now. All their problems evaporated like water thrown onto flames.

THE NEXT MORNING, Sean sat in a chair by the window of the motel and watched Lana get dressed. It was already Wednesday, two days before they had to go back to work. They had an eight-hour trek back to San Diego, but sitting in a car with Lana for that stretch of time was no hardship. They had more than enough to talk about.

As he had predicted, the trip seemed very short, but it was dark when they reached the city proper.

Sean wondered if Lana had really given up the arson investigation. Deep down he knew that it's what she really loved. He wished she would admit it to herself.

"Have you gotten another soil sample?"

Lana said, "No. I'm not supposed to be investigating the arsons anymore."

"Right, Lana. When did you get the sample?"

"I didn't collect a sample. Sienna did."

He was silent for a moment. "Do you think that's a good idea?"

"Do you think that climbing the Golden Gate Bridge was a good idea?"

"Are you trying to prove something to command or are you trying to prove it to yourself."

"What, that I won't back down?"

"I don't know, Lana. You explain it to me."

"These are serial arsons. Bryant won't admit that and now I think he might be involved. How can I in good conscience not keep investigating on my own?"

"You're supposed to be following orders."

"I know that. I can't let this go. It's too important to ignore."

"I'm not arguing with you. I just want to make sure you understand what's going on. Going against Bryant won't be easy and going against command will be even worse."

"I know I have a lot at stake, but it's still my call."

Sean had to admit that it was her call and her business, but he cared about her so that made it his business, too. "I'll always be there for you whenever you need me to be."

"I know that."

"Good, so don't hesitate to ask me."

"I won't."

LANA ENTERED THE TESTING center and took a desk. Other people filed in and took the remaining desks. There wasn't anyone from her squad, which she was thankful for. She really didn't want to face anyone right now. The test was something that was private and she wanted to keep it that way until the list was posted.

By the time eight o'clock rolled around, there were three hundred people filling all available seats.

She'd studied for this, prepared for it and it was the next step in her life-long dream to become captain.

A feeling of being crowded, of being boxed in, moved in on Lana. She closed her eyes, taking a slow breath to keep from getting up and leaving the room. She was just feeling the pressure, she told herself.

But it lingered after she'd completed all the answers on the test. She headed over to the gym and put herself through a workout that had sweat pouring off her. But it didn't release the pressure in her chest.

She was just opening her door when she heard a car pull up. When she turned around, she saw it was her father. That trapped feeling intensified and she pushed the door open and dropped her gym bag on the floor.

She held the door and let her father in. She walked into the living room and sat down on the sofa. "Do you want some iced tea?"

"Sure."

Lana went into the kitchen to pour two glasses.

She walked back out to the living room and handed her father a glass.

"How was the test?"

The knot in her stomach tightened and a headache pressed against her forehead. "It was okay."

He stared at her, and then he released a long breath and glanced around the room. He finally spoke, his tone wary. "Okay? Do you think you passed?"

Lana shrugged and took a sip of tea. She sat down on the sofa. "Yes. I think so. I knew the answers."

"You don't sound too happy about it."

"I'm just tired, Dad. The test went okay."

He looked down and the knot tightened to something painful. She should have put the book in her backpack.

"What's this?" He picked her book up off the coffee table.

"I'm taking a burning patterns seminar." She took the book out of his hand and tucked it into her backpack at the foot of the sofa.

"Arson investigation again?"

Lana struggled for calm, shifted so that the knot in her stomach would loosen, but it didn't. "I told you, Dad. It makes me a better firefighter and will make me a better captain."

His eyes narrowed and he said, "I never hear of you taking leadership seminars or classes."

"That's a good idea. I'll look into that. When did you want to reschedule the tune up for the car?"

"I could do that now, if you like."

"Great. Let me go and change."

Lana rolled her shoulders to release the tension. The mindless task would keep her mind off why she was feeling so caged today. She'd drawn her father away from his questions regarding her arson classes. He would hit the roof if he knew she was investigating arsons on her own, jeopardizing her very career.

He wouldn't understand.

Hell. She didn't understand it herself.

IT WAS SOME TIME LATER when they finished and Lana was now thoroughly exhausted. She said goodbye to her father and headed toward the shower.

Before she could even strip off her clothes, the phone rang.

"Hello,"

"Hello, Lana, it's Kate. I have bad news."

"The accelerants match with the most recent fire?"

"I'm afraid so. Lana, you need to bring this to someone over Bryant's head."

"I'm not supposed to be doing this at all. I just need a few more days. I have another lead."

"You know who's doing this?"

"No, not yet, but I have a hunch. I just haven't had the time to take care of it."

"Right. You took the test today. How did it go?"

"I think I passed. How well I did in the rankings is anybody's guess."

"You studied hard. You deserve this."

"Yeah."

"What does that mean? You sound so dispirited."

"I don't know. I wish I did. All of a sudden, I'm feeling this trapped sensation. I have a knot in my stomach the size of Texas."

"I'd say it was nerves. When you find out the results, everything will be fine."

"I hope so. Thanks for testing the sample for me."

"My pleasure. Good night."

Lana went into the bathroom and lit a few candles. She stripped down to nothing and got beneath the spray with a soft sigh.

She wished that Sean was here, but he'd had as many errands to do as she did before they had to go to work tomorrow. After the lack of sleep last night, the grueling test, the workout, and her father's pointed questions, she wanted to curl up in Sean's arms and simply be at peace.

But peace eluded her as she toweled off and quickly dried her hair. She climbed into bed and tossed around a bit before she finally gave up.

Getting dressed into a sweat suit and grabbing her pressed uniform, she slipped out of her house.

As the night deepened, she parked her car in front of Sean's apartment and got out. At his door, she knocked. He opened it looking cranky and sleep tousled. The moment he saw her, he smiled.

Reaching out, he pulled her inside and Lana felt a peacefulness slide over her as the door closed at her back.

12

LANA SAT OUTSIDE OF STATION 75 debating the wisdom of her actions.

She held the picture in her hand. A really good likeness of the mysterious firefighter. The only way to find out who he was, was to ask. The helmet he wore had the number 75 on it. He had to be part of this station and if he was, then her hunch meant nothing.

She opened the car door and got out. Entering the interior of the station, she stopped the first man she came into contact with.

"Hi, I'm Lana Dempsey from the eighty-second and I'm trying to find out if this guy works at your station. Do you know who he is?"

The man looked down at the picture for a few minutes. "Nope, I don't know this guy. Maybe he transferred out or is on a different shift. He could also be new."

"Maybe," Lana said.

"Why do you need to find him?"

"I'm investigating some arsons and want to question him."

"Sorry, I can't help you."

"Thanks anyway."

Lana hit five more stations, but no one knew the mysterious firefighter.

When Lana walked into work, she was faced with Bryant standing next to the entrance to her captain's office. This couldn't be good.

"Dempsey!" he called as soon as he saw her and with a sinking sensation, she walked toward him.

"Your captain wants to speak with you."

Lana walked in his office and closed the door. Bryant stood outside; she could see him through the glass.

"What are you trying to do, Dempsey? Show me that you don't know how to follow orders?"

"No, sir."

"Then what is it?"

"What exactly is it that Bryant is saying?"

"That you're showing a picture around and butting into his investigation."

"That's true."

"I'm going to have to put a reprimand into your jacket."

"I understand, sir."

"Dempsey, what is it about this case that's gotten you so involved?"

"I'm concerned that Lieutenant Bryant isn't aggressively following every lead."

"In what way?"

"He's ignored the evidence I brought to him about the matching of the accelerants in each case, not to mention that the MO is the same in all three cases."

"How do you know that he's not aggressively investigating this arson?"

"He hasn't announced that this is a serial arson case and has repeatedly told me that I'm off base."

"What expertise do you have to make this accusation?"

"I've taken numerous seminars...."

"I see that now. In fact, if you wanted to, you could apply to be an arson investigator yourself. You have the credentials."

"Frankly, Captain Troy, I'm interested in becoming captain someday. My focus is on that. I took the arson seminars to make me a better firefighter and candidate for captain."

"Have you taken the test?"

"Yes, sir, yesterday."

"If I cut you some slack here regarding a reprimand in your jacket, can you promise—really promise me that you aren't going to continue to investigate and second guess Lieutenant Bryant?"

"With all due respect, sir, no. I can't promise you one hundred percent. My conscience dictates to me what I must do. If I feel that lives are at risk, how can I turn my back?"

"You're leaving me no choice, but to file a reprimand, but I'll hold off if you can bring me definitive proof that you're onto something.''

"Well, I do have this lead. There's a firefighter that keeps turning up in photos and he's supposed to be with the seventy-fifth, but no one there knows him. I've asked around at other stations, but no luck.''

"What makes you think he's involved?''

"The seventy-fifth wasn't at the first or third fires.''

"You've met this man?''

"Yes, after I pulled Sean out of that apartment fire and again at the wharf fire.''

"Get Bryant in here.''

Lana opened the door and gestured to Bryant.

"Dempsey tells me that the photos she received from your office show a mysterious firefighter. Have you followed up with this lead?''

"What mysterious firefighter?''

"Lana, show Bryant the photo.''

Lana pulled the photo from her purse and handed it to Bryant.

"Do you know who this is?''

"No, sir, but there are hundreds of firefighters in San Diego and transfers happen all the time. Doesn't mean he isn't legit,'' Bryant said, but Lana thought she saw recognition in his eyes.

"Could you look into it and follow up with Dempsey's suspicion that the fires are connected?''

"Yes, sir, but what about Dempsey's breach of authority, Captain? She should be punished for her insubordination."

"You let me handle Dempsey, Bryant. You do your job."

"Yes, sir."

They exited the captain's office and Bryant turned to her.

"You think that you can stick your nose into my job and get away scot-free? If I find out that you're investigating again, I'll go above Troy's head. I don't give a damn what he says."

Lana faced him. She pulled the picture out of his hands. "You see this? There is someone out of frame that he's talking to. Do you have the negative?"

"Yes, I have the negative."

"Maybe there's a lead there."

"Maybe," he said grudgingly.

"And maybe there's something to my assertions that these arsons are connected."

"Maybe."

"That's all I wanted in the first place, Lieutenant Bryant was to make sure that this got investigated properly."

"So maybe *I* was a little off base."

"Why don't you send the negative over to the police lab? Kate can blow up the picture and see who this guy is talking to, then if there's nothing there, I'll stop pushing.''

''I'll get the negative to Ms. Quinn. You can stop your pushing, because I tell you. There's nothing there.''

Bryant turned to go. ''Why are you so interested in this investigation?''

''I told you. Lives are at stake, not just civilian lives, but firefighters, too. I feel obligated to do something about it because you weren't.''

''Are you sure you're not after my job?''

Without waiting for an answer he walked away, passing Sean on his way out.

Sean came up to her. ''What was that about?''

''Bryant is finally listening to reason. I think he's going to give this investigation his full attention.''

''What was that he said about you being after his job?''

''An offhand remark. I'm not after his job.''

He narrowed the distance between them until his mouth was dangerously close to hers. Dangerously tempting. Her lungs knotted with the inviting scent of him.

''There wouldn't be anything wrong with that Lana if you were,'' he said quietly.

''I'm not!''

''Okay. Okay. I'm just saying that with you I think the sky is the limit. No need to get testy.''

''I'm not,'' she said a little softer.

"You do need to be careful." Sean took her hand in his.

The fact that every scrambled nerve in her body leaped at his touch had Lana attempting to pull away. His hand tightened around hers, held on as his eyes darkened. "Something tells me we both need to be careful," he added.

Her heart pounded in her head, masking the sounds of their squad members in the kitchen. Its fast, demanding beat muffled the warning that struggled to sound in the far corner of her brain. She needed to step back, get away from this man who made her forget how to breathe.

Her gaze lowered, settled on the mouth that seemed almost sculpted. She'd never wanted anything more in her life than to feel the press of that mouth against hers.

Swamped by emotion, she forced a steadiness into her voice. "I intend to be careful."

"So do I."

Her gaze rose to meet his. "Are we still talking about the investigation?"

"No. It goes way beyond that, and we both know it."

Wary, she shook her head. "I don't—"

"Something profound is happening between us. Something more than friendship, more than lovers."

She opened her mouth, closed it. It was hard to talk with nerves clogging her throat. Hard to take that next step when she knew she hadn't been totally forthcoming with him.

"I didn't tell you about the mysterious firefighter because I didn't have anything to back it up."

"And."

"And I thought you would try to talk me out of going any further with the investigation."

"You must think I can be very persuasive."

"You are." She looked away and bit her lip.

"What?"

"I haven't told anyone this, but do you know that rich developer William Morris?"

"Sure."

"He's buying up the arson properties and turning them into ritzy condos. It makes me wonder."

"About what?"

"Those properties were run-down, but in areas where there's been a rise in property taxes."

"Lucrative real estate."

"Yes. My thoughts exactly. What if he hired someone to torch those places because the owners wouldn't sell or were asking too much?"

"Burned out rubble isn't very valuable."

"Do you think that I should bring this up with Bryant or go talk to the owners myself."

"Lana, Bryant will shy away from stepping on any rich guy's toes."

"That's what I thought."

Pete Meadows popped his head out of the kitchen. "Bacon and eggs. Let's go people."

They sat down at the table and Pete dished up a huge pan of eggs and another one with bacon. Lana reached out and put some on her plate. As she adjusted her chair, her purse hit the floor and the picture of the mysterious firefighter slipped out, landing near Pete's feet.

"What's this?" he bent down to pick it up and Lana saw his eyes sharpen and narrow. "That's John Fisher. Is this an old photo?"

Lana shook her head. "I got this from arson. They took pictures of every site after the fire."

"That can't be."

"Why not?"

"John Fisher washed out of the program about six years ago."

"What happened?"

"He couldn't cut it."

When the alarm went off, there was no more time for conversation. Lana took the picture from Pete as they all headed toward their gear and the engines.

The dispatcher announced it as a full box, meaning the fire was big. From ten blocks away, Lana could see smoke wafting across the rooftops.

The paint factory was fully involved when the engine pulled up; large billows of smoke belched from the roof, and flames had already broken through.

Lana rushed past a probie struggling with his gear and not yet into his air pack. She entered the warehouse next to the paint factory. Its wide, roll-up doors were flung open, and the space was crowded with cardboard boxes. With an ax in one hand and a nozzle in the other, she clambered up the stacks of boxes toward the lathe and plaster wall. Lana knew that if she could get through the wall, she could get water on the fire. She hoped to then advance to its seat.

She chopped at the lathe and plaster, cradling the nozzle between her knees. The wall sheared off easily, revealing metal corrugation underneath. She swung at the metal, but someone yelled behind her.

Sean settled next to her with a chain saw. It was one thing Sean knew and it was the best way to confidently and precisely cut a metal wall. The corrugation sagged with each quick cut. She stood to one side, ready with the nozzle in case there was fire right behind the wall.

When the flames leaped vehemently through the opening, Lana could see that the paint factory was completely enveloped. They couldn't enter there.

Lana knew from experience that if a third alarm wasn't pulled, it would be soon. The loud sounds of exploding paint filled the air. She moved deeper into the warehouse, chopping holes in the corrugation and sending streams of water in.

After searching for a good entrance, Lana and

Sean found a place where the fire wasn't as intense. With four squad members on their tail, they went through the opening.

More paint exploded nearby and Sean ducked, driving down her head, too.

When she could safely move again, she swung her ax toward a large plate glass window. Glass exploded outward and fell to the pavement below. Through the window, Lana could see that thick black smoke blanketed the nearby freeway. Traffic had completely stopped moving.

The upper floor of the paint factory was a large, open space with only skeletal partitions. An open staircase led to a platform above with rudimentary railings. Next to this was an open attic space that gave her and Sean perfect access to the now burning virulent fire below.

With a slightly higher angle on the fire, perhaps the water could douse the fire and salvage some of the owner's property.

The floor was nothing but plywood and Lana walked gingerly across it testing each step for any weakness before she placed her boot.

Slowly they inched closer to the office that obviously had a direct stairway up to the roof. Her radio crackled and her captain told her to clear the way for the squad to reach the roof for ventilation.

Through the smoke and fire, she spied the office door and as she watched she noticed the telltale sign of smoke wafting under the door, then abruptly, being sucked back in.

"Backdraft!" she screamed.

Then someone pushed her out of the way of the door as it exploded outward. The hose caught between her and her body thereby protecting her and anyone else around her. Lana fought to hold on as the hose seemed to squirm with a life of its own.

"Are you okay?" Sean yelled close to her ear.

Lana rose to her feet.

"I'm fine." She turned to look and all her squad members were rising from where they had jumped for cover.

"Good call," a firefighter yelled. Lana couldn't make out who it was because of the smoke and roar of the flames.

Lana's heart lurched thinking what could have happened, but the fire was what was important right now. She shrugged off the incident and pushed forward. She had a mission to clear a path to the roof.

The rest of the fire was a blur. Chopping holes with the large, powerful circular saw, sending in streams of water, steam so thick it obscured a clear view. The building creaked and groaned and cracked. Every so often more paint exploded, sending what looked like fireworks into the air. Timbers gave way with muffled thumps, and the metal corrugation whined as the intensity of the heat bent and melted it. Every so often, too, the air cleared and

Lana could make out the tall and thin wreck of the structure.

Lana and her crew members fought the blaze all afternoon, but the paint factory suffered irreparable damage. The only alternative for the owner would be to rebuild.

Lana went back to the engine and approached the captain. "Do you want me on fire watch tonight?"

"No, we're being relieved by the seventy-fifth. Go back to the station. Good job on the backdraft, Dempsey."

Lana smiled and nodded.

Captain Troy turned to her, his mouth tightening. "Did you see your mysterious firefighter?"

"No. Why?"

"Seems that the fire was started the same way. Accelerant soaked rags in the basement."

Lana looked up at the building and suddenly wanted this to be her case so she could stop tiptoeing around. She felt the same shot of adrenaline she felt when being confronted with a challenge.

"Cap, I'm going to find Sean."

"Make it fast, Dempsey."

Lana headed toward the building, but she didn't look for Sean. Instead, she headed for the office, the potential for a discovery sizzling along her nerve endings.

Parts of the office were still intact after the blast that had almost killed her and her squad members.

What she saw made her pulse increase double-time. Someone had deliberately set up a backdraft, but the question wasn't why? Lana knew whoever had done this was trying to kill firefighters. The question was had she been the target?

"Someone set this deliberately," Sean said.

Lana turned to look at him. "Yes."

"Your mysterious firefighter?"

"John Fisher? I don't know. I didn't see him at this scene."

"If it hadn't been for you, we would all be singing with the angels." Sean rubbed at a smudge of soot on her cheek looking worried and pensive. "Remember how I told you to be careful?"

"Yes."

"Now I think you should. It's too dangerous."

"I don't need you to tell me what to do, Sean. You may have gotten a new lease on life, but that doesn't apply to me. I make my own decisions."

"I'm just saying that in light of this deliberate backdraft, I think you should back down."

"You think this was meant for me?"

"Yes."

"That by investigating this arson, I have put all my squad members in jeopardy."

"Not deliberately."

"If Bryant doesn't do his job, Sean, then what? More firefighters in jeopardy, the public. I can't stop now."

"Then I'm going to be your shadow."

"I don't need a bodyguard."

"Well, you've got one anyway."

"I think this has gone beyond Bryant. I'm giving my information to Sienna."

CALLS KEPT LANA BUSY the rest of her shift, and thankfully there were no more arson incidents.

Just as she was about to walk out of the station to go talk to Sienna, Sean stopped her near her car.

"I want to go with you."

"That's not necessary."

"Lana, I'm worried about you."

"I don't need you following me around 24/7, Sean. I can handle myself and have been for years. Come over for dinner tonight, okay?"

"I don't like it, but all right."

FEELING SAFER AFTER HER VISIT with Sienna, Lana headed home. After some sack time, she went into the kitchen and began to prepare the meal.

She'd had a ball of apprehension lodged in her stomach, and the thought of eating didn't appeal to her. What was the matter with her? Why couldn't she feel relief now that the test was over?

Was she in the process of trashing her career? Why wasn't she more alarmed? Why did the thought of never becoming captain not fill her with panic? It's what she worked her whole life toward.

The soft knocking on the door sent her into the foyer to let Sean in.

She wanted to go into his arms and let him hold her, but that would be giving into her weakness. And she never gave in.

"You okay?" he asked, sliding his hand into her hair and cupping her cheek.

"I'm fine. Dinner is almost ready."

"What are we having?"

"Salmon steaks, rice, salad and a nice bottle of white wine."

"How did it go with Sienna?"

"I told her everything, including the backdraft suspicion."

"What did she say?"

"She's going to pick up John Fisher and consult with Bryant."

"She's a good cop. She'll get the job done."

Lana nodded and pulled the fish out of the oven and dished up two plates. "It's out of my hands now."

Setting them on her small table, she lit the candlesticks and turned off the lights.

"This is nice."

"It is and when I get the kitchen remodeled and painted, it'll be even better."

"The last project for your bungalow."

A demanding knock sounded on the door, startling Lana. She pushed her chair up and went into the foyer. When she opened the door, her father, his face twisted with fury, stalked into the house.

"Dad…"

"What is this I hear about you actively going against orders and investigating arsons?"

Sean came in from the kitchen. When Lana's father saw him, he pointed a finger at him. "And you're still sleeping with a squad member. This is too much, Lana."

Lana felt heat suffuse her face as she glared at her father. Softly she said to Sean, "I'll call you later."

"Lana, are you sure you want me to leave?"

Her father answered for her. "Yes, leave, this is a private conversation between me and my daughter."

"Dad!"

Lana took Sean's arm and led him to the door. "I'll call you later." She kissed Sean on the cheek and opened the door.

He looked at her father and at her. "Call me as soon as you can."

He went out the door and Lana closed it.

"I want an answer, Lana."

"I couldn't ignore the signs."

"You couldn't? Are you willing to take everything you've worked for and throw it away? Do you think you'll get appointed as captain of a station with a reprimand in your jacket?"

"This is too much pressure. Too much. I'm only doing what I think is right. What is wrong with that?"

"I've made my share of mistakes, Lana. I know the score and you should heed what I have to say."

"That's not a very good answer, Dad. All my life I've thought that I wanted to be captain. Now I'm not really sure."

"Are you deliberately trying to damage your record?"

"No. I told you. I'm doing what I think is right. The arson investigator is not doing his job."

"And does that automatically make it your responsibility to buck authority and investigate on your own."

"What would you have me do? Turn my back on potential deaths not only to firefighters, but also to the public? I made an oath to serve and protect. I can't turn my back and pretend. I've tried to hand the evidence over and back out, but nothing is happening, not until I made sure it did. You should be proud of me for standing up for what I believe instead of acting like me not making captain is more important to you than my integrity."

"What is this really about, Lana? Is this squad member you're sleeping with changing your mind? Are you having second thoughts about a career?"

"I don't know. I really don't know what I want anymore."

"I'll tell you what you want. You want to be captain and I don't know what's been going on lately, but you get your head on straight and drop this investigation before it's too late. Sever your ties with this guy, it won't look good if it's discovered that you're having an affair.''

"Stop telling me what to do. I'm sick of it.''

He stood there in shocked silence as if he'd never expected those words from her mouth, but she knew they were true.

"You've taught me to be independent, but have never let me make my own choices.''

"Are you saying that this is my fault? My fault?''

Lana didn't have an answer.

"I've only tried to help you on the path you wanted to go.''

"Have you? Have you really? I don't know what that is anymore.''

"Have you gotten the results from your test? Is the score bad?''

"No, this has nothing to do with the test. It has to do with how I feel inside. Whether my dreams have been my own or something you wanted so desperately and superimposed on me. You couldn't achieve captain, so you decided that your little girl would. Maybe you're not even aware of it yourself, but you've pushed me. I need time to decide what's important to me.''

"After all that I've done for you, I can't believe

this is how you treat me. When you've come to your senses, come see me.''

"Does that mean if I don't choose your path, I shouldn't bother to come see you at all?"

"Make the right decision, Lana."

HER BREATH HEAVED in her lungs, her thighs burned, and her heart pumped frantically as she took the bleachers as if her life depended on it.

Had she been so blind that she couldn't see that becoming captain had never been her dream? Or was she confused? Even in college when she'd wanted to change her major to forensics, her father had talked her out of it. Had she let him or was it what she really wanted?

He'd always been there to steer her back to becoming what he couldn't. Had his dream been riding her for years and as a result had she pushed away her dissatisfaction, denied her feelings, and acquiesced.

She did know that the thought of using chemical tools and observation to bring arsonists to justice thrilled her. She couldn't deny that anymore.

"When are you going to stop?" Sean asked when she got to the bottom of the bleachers.

Irritation slammed through her. When she'd called him and told him that she needed to let off steam and that she'd call him back tomorrow, she didn't expect that he would show up here.

"When I'm ready."

He grabbed her arm. "Lana, you look exhausted. Talk to me."

"Don't tell me what to do."

"What happened with your father?"

Anger burst full force inside her and she paced away from him. "I don't want to talk about that with you. I'm still trying to pick up the pieces of my life right now."

"Right. I get it." He turned and walked away and Lana's heart lurched. She couldn't tell him about this. It was too private, too painful to share with him right now. Why couldn't he understand that?

"Sean," she called and caught up with him. "I'm sorry, but I can't."

"You've been doing that quite a bit lately. Is it because now we're lovers and our friendship isn't quite as *defined* as you want it to be?"

"No. It doesn't have anything to do with that."

"You've always been able to talk to me before. Why is it different now?"

"I don't know. It just is and I can't explain it any better than that."

She watched his retreating back, feeling as if something was slipping through her fingers, something precious and unique, but she couldn't holler for him to come back. She just stood in the cool night and watched the fog roll in off the ocean, feeling as if the murkiness was clouding a lot more than her vision.

13

"WE PUT AN APB OUT ON JOHN FISHER," Sienna said as she walked into Lana's kitchen.

"So you were able to get a warrant for his arrest?"

"Based on the pictures you supplied, yes. We searched his house and discovered accelerants. We also discovered firefighting gear. Lots of it. Kate is analyzing the accelerant and the containers now."

"Have you told Bryant any of this information?"

"Yes, stopped there first."

"Did he give you the negative?"

"What negative?"

Lana pulled the picture out of her bag. "See here. Right at the edge of the photo, someone's been cropped off. I thought it might be useful to find out who he was talking to."

"Right. I'll ask Bryant about this when I see him."

"Thanks for moving on this so quickly."

"Putting an arsonist behind bars is important. One of my best friends is a firefighter after all," Sienna smiled, grabbed a piece of toast off Lana's plate.

"What's wrong?"

"Everything."

"Why didn't you call me?"

"I'm so confused, I don't know how to express what I'm feeling."

"Start at the beginning."

"You know that this arson thing has gotten me into hot water. My father found out and he came over last night, embarrassed me in front of Sean. I sent Sean home and had it out with him."

"What did you say, Lana?"

"That I was tired of him telling me what to do. Now I'm not so sure what I want."

"But you have opportunities, right?"

"Yes."

"Can't go wrong with that. I think you should do what makes you happy, Lana. Don't worry how it affects other people."

"Do you love being a cop?"

"Yes. I can't imagine doing anything else."

"It's not that clear-cut for me."

"It will be, just work it out in your head."

"Then there's Sean."

"What about him?"

"He's changed from my best friend into this le-thal hunk with attitude all over the place. I can't seem to tell him about the test or articulate what's going on with me."

"Lana, your relationship with him has changed entirely. Why don't you give it time?"

"I wish I knew what to do."

"Are you sure it's Sean who's changed?"

"You always ask me the tough questions, Sienna."

"Answer them now, Lana. Believe me. It's best to deal with your emotions now rather than later."

"This dare I pushed you all into. I did it on purpose because I wanted a reason to go after him. I should have left our relationship alone. I don't think he and I can just be friends anymore."

"Discovery is sometimes a violent thing."

"So isn't change?"

"That it is. Listen, why don't you think on it some more and call me if you need me. You got me in on this case and I want to find this guy for you. It worries me that he's on the street."

"Thanks for stopping by."

"How about a movie tonight?"

"I have to work. Got called in and with the overtime I'll have enough to remodel my kitchen."

"The place is coming along beautifully. Be safe and I'll talk to you soon."

Lana sat at her kitchen table and pondered what Sienna had to say and what her father had to say. Maybe he was right. Maybe her confusion stemmed from her closeness to Sean. She did have an obligation to her family. And becoming captain was important. She had been muddled when she'd rebelled against her father and the many years of Dempsey tradition at Station 82. How could she have gone this long wanting something and then decided it wasn't right for her? Sean was the confusing factor in her life. Once she cleared her mind, she would be very sure that becoming captain *was* the right decision for her.

It would be best to transfer to another station. Her father wouldn't like it, but she couldn't ask Sean to do it. It wouldn't be right. A clean break was what she would need to get him out of her system and back on track.

It hurt to think about distancing herself from Sean, but her life had only gotten complicated when their relationship had changed.

SEAN STOOD IN FRONT OF THE LIST and looked at it dumbfounded. Lana's name was at the top. The number one slot. She would be promoted.

Admiration, elation mixed together with dread. In the next minute it got worse as panic circled in his gut. There was a significant reason why Lana hadn't told him about the test. He knew that she had aspirations even though she hadn't voiced them to him.

He'd come to the station to find his misplaced wallet. After looking in his uniform pants, he'd found it. When he'd come downstairs, he saw all the guys milling about and realized that they'd posted the list of the people who'd passed. It was always a source of gossip.

He left the station and drove over to her house. Parking the truck, he got out. She was outside digging in the garden, her dark hair flashing mahogany in the sun. When he walked up to her, she gave him a wistful smile.

"Hi, want some lemonade? I was just about to get myself some. The sun is hot."

"The list is out."

Her reaction made his gut clench as she swallowed hard, then spoke, her voice unsteady. "I was going to tell you."

Sean watched her, a sick feeling unfolding in his belly. "When? When it was a done deal? I'm surprised that you took the test."

"Why?"

"You want to be an arson investigator. I've known it for a long time. You just don't want to admit it to yourself or to your father. You'd be wasted as a captain."

"You don't think I could do the job?"

"Are you kidding me? You'd be very good in that job. But as an arson investigator, you'd kick ass. I've never seen instincts like yours. Lana, you're a natural and San Diego needs arson investigators like you. Captains are a dime a dozen. I can't believe that you don't see it."

When she made no response, he hunkered down to be at the same level with her. She sat back on her heels. He watched her for a moment, then spoke, his tone still quiet. "I think maybe it's time you leveled with yourself, Lana."

She shot him a sharp glance, and then she turned back to the flower she was planting, her jaw set. "Yes, I think investigating fires is interesting," she said, patting the dirt around the seedling. "But you're wrong about what I want to do with my life. I'm dedicated to becoming a captain. It's what I want. And I'm beginning to think he's right. I shouldn't be sleeping with a squad member that I would someday command."

His expression grim, Sean looked away. He waited a minute, then looked at her and spoke, "Don't you think that's between you and me?"

More silence and his stomach fell like a stone.

"It's more than that. It's also about how our relationship is different."

"Sean…"

"I should have seen it. I'm such a fool. I thought we were drawing closer and all this time you were holding out on me because you're afraid of making a change. It scares you to realize that what you worked for isn't what you want. You don't want to disappoint your father."

"I really don't know what you're talking about.

I know what I want. You may have gotten all assertive on me, Sean, but don't tell me what I want.''

She stared at him, a sad look in her eyes, her arms clutched in front of her, and something hard and cold settled in the pit of Sean's stomach. He stared at her, then turned his head and clenched his jaw in disgust. After all this time, he had never put it together until now. And he didn't like it one damned bit. ''I see that you're caught between your own desires and your father's expectations. It's a hard place to be.''

She seemed frozen in place, her eyes wide and wounded, and he looked away and shook his head, his frustration compounding. He waited until he got a grip on the feelings building inside him, then he faced her again. ''I'm not your father, Lana. I'm not going to coerce or manipulate you into something you don't want to do. I'm also not going to stand here and cover up the truth because you don't want to hear it.''

She never said a word. She just stood there, huddled in the warmth of her arms, but he saw the answer in her despairing eyes as clearly as if she'd spoken it.

Sean stared at her, then shook his head and gave her a tight smile. He loved her so much. He could tell her that and complicate her life some more, but ultimately Lana had to make her own decision.

"Okay. We don't sleep together. I accept that, but don't shut me out, Lana."

"I'm transferring."

"What?"

"Sean, it's for the best this way."

So this was it. And there wasn't a damn thing left for him to say.

AFTER HER DOUBLE SHIFT, Lana knocked on Captain Troy's office door.

"Come," he said brusquely. He smiled when he saw it was her. "Dempsey. Come in and I hear congratulations are in order."

"Thanks, sir. I'm here to make a request."

"Shoot."

"I'd like a transfer to a different station."

He frowned. "Are you having problems here, Dempsey?"

"No. I feel that it's time for me to go. With my new promotion and my record, I feel it's time for a change."

"All right, but I hate to lose you. Put it in writing…"

"I already have." With a lump in her throat and her chest tight, she handed it to him.

"When would you want to go?" he asked, glancing down at the request.

"As soon as possible."

"All right. I'll call you with the particulars."

"I do want to say that serving under you has been a pleasure, sir."

"We're going to miss you. There's been a Dempsey at this station for three generations."

14

WHEN LANA AND THE SEVENTY-SEVEN pulled up to the fire, a man was waving his arms from a third-floor window.

She was out of the engine as soon as it stopped, directing squad members to get a ladder up to the window. Without hesitation, they got to work and the man was down and away from danger in minutes.

She looked up at the building. It seemed strange to face the foe without Sean at her back, but the transfer was the answer that she needed. She was a leader now. A place she strived for all her life.

She turned on her air pack with one hand, gripped her ax with the other. She could smell the smoke. People were streaming down the stairs. She passed people covering their mouths and coughing. On the second floor, the engine crew turned left, dragging the hose down the hallway. It was filled with a thin gauze of smoke, but there were no visible signs of fire yet. The tension in the air was palpable.

These hotels made Lana nervous. They were old, ramshackle, and shabby, making them dangerous firetraps. Despite the narrow hallways and small boxlike rooms, these hotels were deceptively large. The same brown doors and yellow wall went on forever, confusing and disorienting.

Lana knocked impatiently on each door. If it was locked, she turned her back to it and brought her leg forward. Then she crashed it into the door, which gave way easily.

After checking thoroughly inside, Lana couldn't find anybody, so she went back out into the hallway. She saw the illuminating glow. By now, the engine crew and its hose were out of sight and heading in the wrong direction, and she realized that she had to get another line up here fast. She'd found the fire.

She turned and in her path stood Pete Meadows. He had his ax out swinging toward her head before she could call out. The blow knocked her into the wall and the lights winked out as if someone had turned a switch.

SEAN FINISHED REFILLING the engine with extra SCBAs and turned. Sienna was standing there.

"Sean, I'm looking for Pete Meadows."

"Why?"

"I went to talk to Dane Bryant and caught him packing his car for a long trip. He's in custody for conspiracy to commit arson."

"What does this have to do with Pete?"

"Bryant, Meadows and Fisher were all probies

together. Pete is conspiring with William Morrison to torch old buildings and then Morrison buys them for a song.

"The negative, which was on Bryant when we apprehended him, shows Pete talking to Fisher at the first fire scene. Bryant told us that Meadows paid him to botch the investigation."

Kate was standing next to her. "Where's Lana?"

"She doesn't work at this station anymore. She took a transfer. Why?"

"We found Fisher dead," Sienna said.

"It looks like he committed suicide with a note and everything," Kate added.

"But you don't believe it?"

"No. The angle of the shot is all wrong. I noticed it immediately and told Sienna."

"You think Pete is behind this?"

"Bryant says that Pete killed Fisher because he was a liability. That's what spooked Bryant into running. He was afraid of Meadows."

Panic put a vise grip around Sean's heart. "Let's find Meadows quick."

They searched through the station, but Pete wasn't there.

"Can you find out where Lana is?" Sienna said with a worried frown.

Sean walked into the captain's office. The captain called the dispatcher and handed the address over to Sean.

After Sean grabbed his gear, they headed for Sienna's car at a run. They drove to the apartment fire.

Sean, Sienna and Kate rushed up to one of the firefighters, and Sienna spoke. "We're trying to find Lana Dempsey. Police business," she said showing her badge.

The firefighter turned his head to speak into his mike. "Dempsey, get your butt out here. There's a cop who wants to speak with you."

They waited a beat, but the radio remained silent. "Casey, is Dempsey with you?"

"Sure, she's right...she was here a minute ago. The fire's getting bad and we might have to pull out. We're running out of hose."

"Can you not see Dempsey?" the firefighter barked.

Sean was already donning his gear. Sienna and Kate rushed after him. Sean stopped them. "You can't go in."

"Find her. Please," Kate said as Sienna silently pleaded with her eyes.

"Don't worry. I will."

LANA CAME TO SLOWLY AWARE of the black, like a wide hot sea, the heat brushing against her in waves. Water fell from above, searingly hot, sneaking into her collar and trickling down her back. Orange flashes sparked above her, fleeting shadows of color. She was still in the hallway and if the fire got over her or behind, she would be trapped. Maybe that was what he had in mind.

Lana realized that her SCBA was gone. She coughed as she breathed in the hot tang of the smoke, making her eyes water.

She looked up as Pete watched the fire lick at the wood above him.

"Pete, what are you doing?"

"Making sure that you pay for meddling in my very lucrative affairs. You're too damn smart, Lana."

"It was you all along, you were framing Fisher and bribing Bryant."

"Right on both accounts. Bryant is greedy and disgruntled. He was easy. I gave John gear and a scanner so he could keep track of when we went on calls. He was so eager to be a firefighter. Not quite right in the head."

"Sienna will figure this out."

"No she won't because John can't tell her anything with a bullet in his brain. Everything points to him, including pictures of him at the scene. When I overheard you talking to O'Neill about the Morrison connection, I knew I had to do something before you told that cop friend of yours."

"So your amorous attention was all a smoke screen."

"That's right. You're not really my type. I like obedient blondes."

"Why did you do it, Pete?"

"I wish I could say I had these terrible pent-up feelings, but the truth is, I did it for the money."

He advanced on her with the ax and Lana dodged as he swung it toward the wall where she was sitting. It hit the wall with a terrible thud and Lana coughed as she swallowed more smoke.

"Sorry about this, Lana. Guess you won't get to be captain someday."

And suddenly, blindingly, Lana realized that she didn't want it. What she wanted was a life with Sean. Now she was afraid that she'd never get a chance to tell him.

She loved him with all her heart.

Sitting in the hallway, wondering what Pete would do next reminded her that life was fragile and precious, that there were things worth keeping, worth being a little more careful for. That life was full of small miracles easily lost.

She learned that courage didn't reside in physical danger. Courage means confronting fears and doubts and making the right choice, taking a stand and stating what it is that she wanted in life. It wasn't the same thing her father wanted.

What she wanted more than anything was to get out of this hallway, this escalating inferno and tell her father how she felt. Tell Sean how she felt.

Pete moved closer to her and hunkered down. "Don't fight it, Lana. You can't win."

Lana moved her hand around the floor trying to find something, anything with which to defend herself. But Pete was moving, rising and bringing his ax up.

SEAN MOVED AS FAST AS POSSIBLE through the smoky building. As he passed crews, he asked about Lana, but no one had seen her or knew where she was. He started to climb, his heart beating hard. How stupid could he have been to let her walk away from him? He couldn't live without her. He wanted the chance to hold her in his arms and tell her how much she meant to him. He loved her. With grim determination, he started taking the steps two at a time.

LANA DUCKED THE AX AGAIN and rolled away. Her head was still woozy and the lack of oxygen didn't help. She grabbed the big flashlight off her belt. With a scream, she rushed Pete as he was trying to pull his ax out of the wall.

She hit him a glancing blow to the temple and without waiting to see if he went down, she ran for the stairs. Just as she reached the top stair, he grabbed the back of her jacket and pulled hard. She went down and hit her head. The room spun and she could barely make out his sooty face in the glow from the encroaching fire as he swung the ax up.

A howling call came out of the darkness of the stairwell and then a huge force flew over her and into Pete. Lana rolled onto her side and tried to get up, tried to help the man who had come to her rescue. But she couldn't seem to make her body work.

Then in that same red glow, she saw it was Sean. She wanted to yell to him, tell him, but all that came out of her throat was a croak. They grappled near the banister, Pete pushing Sean against the wooden barrier that groaned and popped as wood loosened beneath the weight. Suddenly, Sean turned and with a mighty heave threw Pete away from him and against the banister. With a final groan, the wood gave way and Pete fell into the blackness.

Sean's face loomed over hers and she reached up to touch his skin, feel the heat of him.

"Hang on," he said hoarsely, pulling off his mask to give her oxygen.

Sean wasn't only her squad member, friend and lover.

He was her life.

Lana closed her eyes and the clear, pure air entered her lungs and she let the darkness settle over her as gently as a blanket.

SEAN DONNED THE MASK, his heart in his throat when he saw that Lana had passed out. Then Sean ran out of time. Fire surrounded them on all sides, ravenous and crimson, unbelievably hot. He gathered Lana into a fireman's carry as fire sped across the floor, consuming fuel and air like something alive.

Fear like he'd never known before sank rending claws into his stomach, tearing at his throat. They were trapped, fire writhing on either side of them. Determined, he fought through the fear.

Fire in a great wall of snapping, writhing flames blocked his exit to the stairs. If he didn't act, the roaring heat that surged toward them would engulf them.

His SCBA started whistling, and he cursed it. He wasn't going to die and he wasn't going to let Lana die. He took a deep breath, tightened his hold on Lana and jumped into the jaws of the beast.

For a split second he was in the fire's embrace, grasping flames, heat so intense, he could barely breathe.

They emerged on the other side into thick black smoke. Groping for the stair railing that would lead him down to safety, Sean knew it was blind luck when his gloved hand felt the wood.

Smoke was swelling up the stairwell, rising like a huge black balloon. Lana coughed hard against his back, the vibrations reaching even through his thick turnout coat.

He pulled her off his shoulders, leaning her against the wall while he stripped off his mask.

Overcome by smoke and sliding into shock,

Lana's knees buckled and Sean had to catch her against him and hold her.

"Lana, hang on. Don't give up," he yelled at her as he heaved her back over his shoulder.

He jogged down the steps taking them two at a time, descending as fast as he could. He lost count of the flights. Lana was still unconscious, her head lolling, her arms limp. His eyes stung from the thick smoke. His lungs felt on fire, but he didn't slow. All he knew was that he had to get her to safety.

She was still out as he passed firefighters rushing past him with hoses.

The smoke had thinned considerably by the time he got to the front doors and lurched through.

He heard the shouts. His vision blurred as Sienna rushed up to him along with Kate. Two paramedics were close behind.

"Oh God, Sean," Kate said.

"Oxygen." Not relinquishing his hold on her, he shrugged off their hands and moved farther away from the flaming building and into the street.

He headed for the closest ambulance and grabbed at the oxygen tank. "Oxygen," he croaked. "Hurry." His throat closed up and a spasm of coughing tore at his lungs as he gently set her down on a stretcher.

Her face was so still. He couldn't tell if she was breathing. A burly paramedic muscled him aside and fitted an oxygen mask over her face.

"Is she all right?" Wiping away tears with the back of her hand, Kate grabbed Sean's shoulder.

Sienna asked frantically, "Is she breathing?"

The tension left Sean's body when he saw her chest rising and falling. He closed his eyes and sank to his knees beside the stretcher.

When the stretcher lifted, Sean rose.

"You can't ride in here," the paramedic insisted.

Sean pushed the man against the side of the ambulance. "Just try to keep me out."

"Okay, okay. Let's go."

WHILE RIDING THROUGH THE CITY, watching everything the paramedics did, he breathed in oxygen in great gulps, but his lungs still felt gritty and raw.

When they got to the E.R., Sean tried to go with her, but a nurse grabbed his arm and directed him toward an examining room.

He tried to fight her, but the room started spinning and he found himself flat on his back.

"Be still," a big doctor instructed him, standing above him.

"Lana…"

"Your friend is in good hands. So stop squirming or I'll have to stick you with a needle to quiet you down."

Sean quieted down. He didn't want to be sedated. He wanted to see Lana. So he let the doctor clean him out and give him some more oxygen.

"How is she?"

"I don't know."

"Could you please find out?"

"Will you stay put for a few minutes until I get back?"

"Yes, just let me know how she is and I'll stay here like a good boy."

The doctor disappeared and when she came back she said, "Your friend has smoke inhalation and a concussion from a blow to the head," she stated. "And she's in shock. That wins her rest and relaxation with twenty-four-hour care."

Sean breathed a sigh of relief.

SEAN REFUSED TO BE ADMITTED. Ignoring the doctor's caution that he should also stay, he went out into the waiting area. Sienna and Kate sprang up from their chairs the moment they saw him.

"Lana?" They asked in unison.

"They're working on her," Sean said, giving both women a hard hug. He nodded to A. J. Camacho, standing at Sienna's shoulder.

"They wouldn't give us much information because we're not family," Kate said. "Fat lot they know."

"She's like a...no she's our sister."

Taking a deep breath, Sienna slipped her hand into A.J.'s and sat down.

Sean sat, too, still feeling woozy.

Kate said, "You saved her life."

"Thank God," Sienna said.

A.J. put his arm around her and drew her close, saying, "It's okay, sweetheart."

She turned her face into his chest and relaxed against him and Sean suddenly wanted what they had found. Wanted it with Lana.

As they sat there in silence waiting for news of Lana, the squad began to trickle in. Firefighters who hadn't even bothered to go back to the station after the fire was extinguished. They crowded around Sean, patting him on the back and giving him their thanks for saving Lana. Then his squad started arriving one by one until the hospital was crowded with San Diego firefighters.

"Mr. O'Neill?" The nurse approached him. "The doctor said you can see your friend for a few moments."

They all came to their feet and Sean said, "How is she?"

"She's stabilized, and sedated," the doctor said, looking around at all the faces.

He glanced back at all the people who had come to make sure Lana was all right. His gaze zeroed in on Kate and Sienna. "I'll come back and tell you how she is."

Lana's room was private, and dimly lit. She lay very still, very pale, but her hand, when he took it in his was warm.

"Do you think you're going to stay?" the nurse asked in a hushed voice.

"Get used to the idea, lady."

After she was gone, Sean pulled the chair up to the side of the bed and sat with Lana's hand in his.

He sat and watched her face, the rise and fall of her chest.

After a little bit a nurse asked him to wait outside while she checked Lana's vital signs and changed her IV.

Sean left the room and was greeted with Lana's father hurrying down the hallway with her sister Paige and her fiancé Justin following close behind.

"Where is she?" her father demanded.

Sean pointed toward the room he just came out of.

Without another word, they all moved past him and inside.

AFTER ASSURING KATE and Sienna, Sean walked to the small hospital chapel and sat in the last row. He shut his eyes and let his mind close down.

"I didn't expect to find you here," Lana's father whispered from behind him.

"Didn't expect to be here," Sean said, moving over so the man could sit down.

"I wasn't sure you would even want to talk to me, young man."

"Why?"

"Well, the last time I talked to you, I wasn't exactly cordial."

With a short laugh, Sean said, "No, you weren't."

"I apologize for that. I want the best for my daughter."

"And living out your dream? Is that best for her?"

"It's what she wants."

Sean nodded. "That's what she told me."

"You don't believe her?"

"I think that she thinks it's true, but deep down inside, she has dreams of her own."

"Maybe," Mr. Dempsey said softly, as he turned and walked away.

WHEN LANA WOKE IN THE MORNING, she turned her head on the pillow to find Sean, his upper torso resting on the bed beside her.

She reached out and caressed his face and his eyes fluttered opened. He was instantly awake and on his feet.

"How do you feel?" He put up his hand. "Wait, don't answer that. Your throat is going to be very raw and very sore for a while."

Her head throbbed and she reached up to touch her forehead.

"That's where Pete must have hit you."

"What happened to him? He fell." Her voice was a raspy croak.

"He's dead."

"Oh."

"He almost killed you."

"I know, but it doesn't stop me feeling sorry for him."

"Lana, you are too generous."

"Maybe," she said.

"No doubt about it," he said and buried his face in her hair.

She was feeling the effects of the sedative in her system as she drifted closer to sleep.

As she floated, losing her grip on consciousness, she heard Sean say, "It's one of the reasons why I love you so much."

LANA WAS WAITING PATIENTLY in bed for her father's arrival. He was bringing her clothes to her. She was being released today. "Come in."

Sienna and Dane Bryant's boss, Lieutenant Jason Wright came into the room.

Sienna hugged Lana. "It's good to see you looking so good, but are you sure you're ready to leave?"

"I've gotten a clean bill of health, but have to stay home another week before they'll clear me for duty." She turned to Jason. "It's a surprise to see you here, Lieutenant Wright."

"I heard about your investigating skills, Lieutenant Dempsey, and I wanted to offer you a job. I have a vacancy as you know."

Lana chuckled. "I heard that."

"Bryant took a deal. He pled guilty in exchange for giving up Morrison. Dane's sentencing is next week. I've got a feeling he won't be getting out for a long time. The grand jury has also indicted William Morrison. With Dane's testimony and Jericho's prosecution, I think Mr. Morrison will also become a guest of the state," Wright explained.

There was another knock on the door and Lana's father came into the room.

"Thanks for bringing me clothes, Dad, and the other things I needed." She was eager to get out of the hospital to confront Sean about what she thought she heard him say. He hadn't been back to see her and she missed him.

"We should get going, Lana," Sienna said as her and Lieutenant Wright said their goodbyes and left.

While she was getting dressed, she thought long and hard about what she was going to say to Sean. But before she made her peace with him, she had to do so with her father.

When she came out of the bathroom, she said, "I need to talk to you."

"About what?"

"The rest of my life."

"I was wondering when we were going to get around to this."

"I want to be an arson investigator."

"Sounds like you'll make a damn fine one."

She opened her mouth to give him all the reasons why she wanted to chuck her—no his—lifelong dream when the words registered. "What?"

"Your friend Sean told me that I was the one pushing you to become something you didn't want to be. I've thought about this a lot while you were in the hospital and realize that he's right. I'm sorry."

She sighed softly, a boatload of weight lifted from her shoulders. It was something to have her father finally understand who she was. She went to him and as he rose, she slipped her arms around his waist. "Thank you, Daddy. I love you."

"I suppose you'll want a ride over to your old station."

"Why?"

"That's where O'Neill is and I think you two need to talk."

"I agree."

"That's something, two agreements in one day."

LANA'S FATHER PULLED UP in front of Station 82 and Lana felt a twinge of homesickness for the place, but she had a job offer for something she really wanted to do and it was time for her to take what she wanted. She got out of the car.

Her father asked, "Do you want me to wait?"

"No, Dad. I think I can get Sean to give me a ride."

"All right. Good luck."

She walked into the station, smelling the familiar smells and seeing the familiar objects.

She heard a cell phone ring then Sean's voice. "Hey, little brother."

There was dead air as Sean listened. "No, Riley, it's time you took responsibility and did it yourself."

There was a pause. "That's right. I have changed. I'm not going to be good old Sean anymore. I'm taking time for myself. You could also start doing some things for Mom." Another pause. "That's the right answer, Riley. I'll see you this weekend. That's right, I'm still holding you to that promise. You'll have to pick up Grammy."

She could hear him chuckling as he disconnected the call.

She rounded the big pumper engine and stopped short. Sean was bent over. His suspenders were loose around his hips and his shirt was off, draped over the front seat. Sweat glistened off his torso as he rubbed at a side panel buffing it to a red glossy sheen.

"Did I hear right? Sean O'Neill saying no to his family."

He froze and then rose, turning to face her. He

looked her up and down as if to make sure she was okay.

"Why aren't you in bed?"

"I've been discharged."

"You're not ready to leave the hospital."

"Do you have a medical degree now, O'Neill?"

"No, but you had a concussion."

"Maybe if you had visited me, you would have seen that I've healed."

He remained silent, setting down the rag.

"Why did you stay away?"

"I didn't want to crowd you."

"You said you loved me."

"I did. I do."

"I missed you."

His eyes lit up, but then he sobered. "I told you. I didn't want to crowd you. I think I've been doing that too much lately."

"You have changed." She smiled. "Bad boy, O'Neill."

"Guess I got sick of being your buddy. Wanted to be something more."

"You are. You're my best friend."

His shoulders slumped, his face falling.

She smiled, "And my lover."

He perked up, but only a little.

"You are greedy."

He stepped closer. "What are you saying?"

"I love you. I love you so much it hurts."

"I love you, too." He gently brought her against him and buried his face in her hair. "Damn, Lana, I've never been so scared."

"Me, either." She rubbed the back of his neck. "But we survived."

"I wasn't going to let you die." Struggling for composure, he eased away.

"You carried me through fire." She shook her head quickly, before he could speak. "If you hadn't I would never have gotten to tell you that you were right. I was afraid. I knew that if I talked about the test with you that it would come out that I didn't want to take it. I do want to be an arson investigator. I've wanted it for years now. I was wrong to shut you out. You make me see things I don't want to see. I didn't want to fail you or my father, but it seems that I couldn't have both of you. If I did what he wanted me to do, I would have disappointed you. If I did what you wanted me to do—what I wanted to do, I would have disappointed him."

Sean shook his head. "You wouldn't have disappointed me, Lana. I only want what makes you happy. You've got to know that your father wants that, too."

"He's already told me. I gave him the truth and he's accepted it. He does want me to be happy. I don't want to lose you, Sean. We can work everything out."

"Yes, we can. Hold on to me, Lana, and never let go."

She slipped her arms around his neck and pressed her mouth to his. He tasted like passion and heat; he tasted like her best friend. He tasted like the man she wanted to spend the rest of her life with.

"There's one more thing," he said. "I know that you have this dare going."

"Sean, that isn't important."

"Sure it is. You were bold enough to make the dare."

"And you have something for me?"

"I sure do, but if you want this souvenir, you'll have to take it off my body."

She laughed. "What is it?"

He went to his locker and retrieved a small box. "They gave this to me for saving you." He opened it and inside was his medal of valor.

"Sean, no."

"Yes." He took out the medal and pinned it to his shirt. "Take it, Lana. It's yours, like my life and my love."

Sighing softly, she whispered against his mouth, "I'll take that dare."

* * * * *

Don't miss the next Woman Who Dares...

Kate's story is coming in January 2004
in MINE TO ENTICE Blaze 119!